BOOK ONE IN THE
IRON BREAKERS TRILOGY

IRON BREAKERS

STAG'S RUN

BY
ZAYA FELI

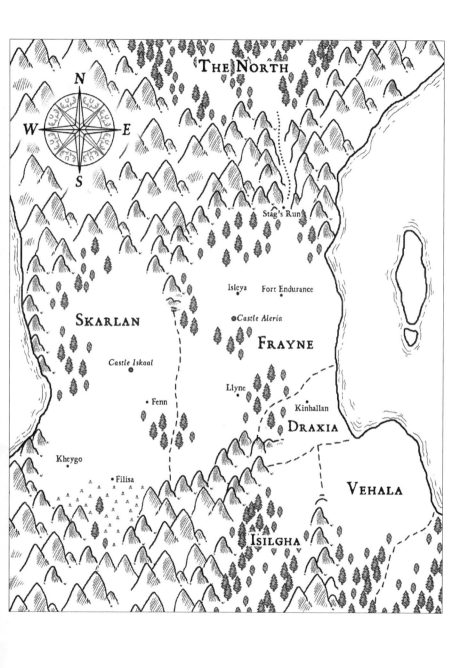

CHAPTER ONE

"Cut it off on the left. Hurry!"

The boar thundered through the undergrowth, two horses close behind it, their tails streaming with their speed. Heat radiated off Ren's grey mare as he reined her to the side, into the path of the boar. The beast turned onto a narrow forest trail and Ren pulled his horse around it to cut it off before it could escape. He ducked his head under low branches, startling a flock of birds that darted from the trees as he raced past. Trees and branches whipped past and gave way to a sunlit clearing as they galloped over the ridge.

Ren hefted his spear. The boar was right in front of him. He had a clear shot. Looking over his shoulder, he saw Hellic's horse clear the trees behind them.

1

Ren lowered his weapon and pushed his mare harder, both of them panting as they sped past the boar, forcing it to stop and turn back towards the horse and rider behind it.

The beast was small, half the size of the larger breeds that roamed these woods, but it was fast and its tusks were sharp. It turned, seemed to size up the other horse, its path blocked in both directions. A second passed in which it seemed to decide whether to charge or run.

It charged.

"Hellic, now!" Ren shouted, forcing his horse in close, a tight grip on his spear in case Hellic missed his shot.

Hellic's aim was true. The spear went deep. Hellic's horse stomped its hooves and tossed its head as he pushed with all his weight against the end of the spear. Finally, the boar went still and sank to its knees. A beautiful, swift kill.

"Excellent," Ren exclaimed, leaning sideways in the saddle to grip and shake Hellic's shoulder in excitement. "Look at those tusks."

Hellic beamed with pride and patted his gelding on the neck. "It's going to taste amazing slow-roasted." His smile was wide, but then it faded and he dragged his eyes from the boar to meet Ren's gaze with a guilty expression. "Sorry. I'll stop talking about it."

Ren shook his head, bringing his horse to a stop next to Hellic's before sliding out of the saddle. "It's all right. I just can't believe King Callun is sending me away," he said, unable to keep all the disappointment out of his voice. "I mean, a trade meeting? Really? Fishing rights can't possibly be that important." Ren grabbed the boar by the tusks, lifting his head up to inspect where Hellic's spear had gone through. Through the neck and straight into the chest.

Hellic dismounted and knelt next to him. "We can celebrate when you get back," he said. "Just the two of us. Wine, good food, slaves." Hellic offered him a smile and Ren mirrored it. He didn't want to be the one to ruin the mood.

Hellic let himself drop back onto the grass, folding his legs. "It should be you on the throne. I don't feel ready for it. You're the oldest."

Ren stood, retrieved a cloth from one of his saddle bags and handed it to Hellic so he could wipe his spear clean of blood. Raising his hand to his lips, he took a deep breath and whistled. "Nobody wants a bastard for a king," Ren reminded him, holding a hand up to shield his eyes from the sun, scanning the treeline. "And I have no complaints about that. Kingship sounds like an awful lot of work. You like hard work, don't you? You'll be a great king." Ren smirked at Hellic and the younger boy rolled his eyes.

From between the trees, a third horse and rider appeared.

"Niklas, over here," Ren called, waving a hand in the air. The rider waved back and steered his horse towards them.

"Whoa, what a beast," Niklas said as he approached, leaning over the side of his saddle to take a closer look at the boar. A wide smile deepened the dimples in his cheeks. "Who took it down?"

"I did," Hellic said. He pushed to his feet and seemed to grow several inches from sheer pride.

Ren smiled to himself at the sight of it, patting Hellic on the shoulder. "All right, let's get it home before we give your father another set of worry wrinkles."

Together, they lifted the boar onto the back of Niklas' horse. Niklas retrieved lengths of rope from his bags and Ren helped him tie the slain boar to the saddle.

"It's heavier than it looks," Niklas groaned, tugging on the ropes to make sure the boar would stay in place. The comment, Ren noticed, only seemed to make Hellic stand taller.

With the boar occupying Niklas' saddle, he and Ren rode together on Ren's mare. The ride back was uncharacteristically quiet. Ren's thoughts kept circling back to the party he would miss and the half day of sea travel ahead of him. The last time he had been on a boat, he had sworn to never do it again. Or at least, to abstain from eating an entire roast chicken before boarding. It hadn't tasted nearly as good on the way up.

Niklas' patience only lasted as far as to the dirt track leading the way back towards the city. "Hey," he said, leaning over to try and catch Hellic's gaze and almost dragging Ren out of the saddle

4

with him. "Cheer up, birthday boy. The party is going to be great and you just took down the king of the forest. Why are you two acting like someone just died?" He poked Ren in the ribs.

Ren couldn't help but smile at the comment, batting Niklas' hand away. The dwarf boar was hardly the king of the forest.

Hellic flushed and nudged his horse to keep it from lagging behind. "Why do you think the Skarlan king wants to come to my birthday celebration?" he asked, a strand of dark hair falling over his eyes as he let his head hang. "They don't like us and we definitely don't like them."

Ren tried for an encouraging smile. "You're turning twenty. That's a big deal. You could legally become king, now. I guess it makes sense for royal families to visit each other for such occasions," he said, not entirely sure if he believed his own theory.

"A king needs a queen," Hellic said darkly.

The terrain sloped downwards. Around them, forest birds sang heartily, completely unfazed by their prince's sour mood.

Niklas laughed. "Such optimism. I thought you liked women."

"I do," Hellic protested. "But haven't you heard what the court has been whispering? They say the Skarlan king wants to offer his daughter to me. I don't want to marry a Skarlan." Hellic's face twisted into a grimace.

"Calm down," Ren said, turning his horse down the trail that led back to the city. "Your father will never marry you to a

5

Skarlan. He hates them as much as anyone."

"I hope you're right."

Ren was about to speak again when the blare of a horn tore through the silence, deep and mournful. They all stopped and listened.

"Here, take the reins," Ren said, passing them back to Niklas before he swung his leg over his mare's neck and dropped onto the ground.

Heading for a collection of large rocks, Ren leapt onto the lowest one, placed his right foot in a crevice, and dragged himself higher until he had a clear view of the valley that stretched out before them. Holding up a hand to shield his eyes from the sharp, early morning sun, he looked out over the city below.

The forest path wound its way to the city of Aleria and the castle within its walls that seemed to shine with a golden glow in the sunlight. To the south lay the royal highway, the main traffic route to and from the capital of Frayne, fringed by neatly kept beech trees and surrounded by green hills.

Even from this distance, Ren could see the grey and silver banners with the howling wolf crest snapping in the wind. Lines of guards riding in formation boxed in what Ren could only assume was the Skarlan king and his daughter riding in the centre. They weren't in a carriage as was the Fraynean custom, but on horses of their own, followed by yet more guards and several supply wagons. They moved towards Aleria like a colony of ants, the horses kicking up clouds of dust that settled on the wheat fields around them.

Ren ran a hand through his hair and blew out a breath, a brisk breeze tugging on his dark green hunting jacket.

"What can you see?" Niklas shouted up at him.

Leaning over the edge of the steep rock, Ren peered over the edge. Niklas and Hellic looked small below. "Trouble," he called back.

* * *

"They're early," Hellic noted, voice tense.

People bowed respectfully as they rode past farms and fields and through the golden city gates. The Fraynean guards in gold and white saluted their crown prince and the queen's bastard, but neither Hellic nor Ren paid them any mind. The white banners with the golden stag's head, Frayne's royal crest, billowed in the wind all along the wide street that led up to the castle gates.

"It's a long journey from Iskaal to Aleria. Maybe they were just eager for some good food and soft beds," Ren said with a shrug.

In front of them, people moved out of their way, steering horses and carriages off the road. Men and women bowed deeply and children hung out of windows to wave at them as they rode past. Ren offered them joyful smiles and blew a young girl a kiss that made her blush bright red and flee back into her house. The friendly attention of the crowd and their softly muttered well-wishes almost made Ren forget about his own displeasure at missing the party. Bastard or not, Aleria loved all of their young, royal stags, even if Ren's golden hair and light blue eyes made him stand out from the rest of the family. Still, there was a certain apprehension in the gathered crowd. In the hundreds of years since the war began, no member of the Skarlan royal family had set foot within the walls of the city without a sword in hand.

"I bet King Halvard wants to talk wedding arrangements with Father before the party," Hellic said, visibly shivering.

Ren couldn't help but feel a sting of sympathy for him. Hellic was bright, smart, and kind. His twentieth birthday was a major affair and Ren had looked forward to celebrating him with the rest of the city all year. King Callun's decision to send Ren off to negotiate trade agreements with the lord of the Isle of Moraen had come completely out of the blue three weeks ago. Ren had been outraged. He could negotiate trades any other day of the year; there was no reason for it to be on his brother's birthday. But the king had been adamant, and no matter what Ren said, he wouldn't budge. It felt like a punch in the face. Ren had searched his memory for anything he might have done to anger the king, but could think of nothing. Now, Hellic had to face their unpleasant guests from the neighbouring country without Ren at his back. Ren couldn't think of a worse way to celebrate a birthday.

"I don't know why Father even let them come," Hellic continued sourly, ignoring the people around them calling out congratulations and praising them on their impressive kill. The streets of the upper district had been lavishly decorated. Gold and white ribbons cascaded down the front of buildings and flowers bobbed in bowls of water on stairs and doorsteps. The large, open space surrounding Frayne's old, circular sanctuary building that on any other day was the scene of the city's largest marketplace, had been vacated, swept and tidied.

"I don't think you can really turn down a king," Ren said, smiling at a woman holding up her young daughter who waved both hands in the air in greeting.

"Father is a king, too!"

From behind Ren, Niklas laughed. "You don't want to start another Frayne-Skarlan war over a birthday invitation, do you?"

Whatever Hellic was going to say in answer was cut off when a massive chestnut war horse came down the street towards them and stopped in their path, its hoof beats loud against the cobblestones.

Berin, captain of the Royal Guard, bowed to them from his saddle.

"Prince Hellic, your father wants you back home at once. Everything is on its tail thanks to our early arrivals," Berin said, panting like he had just run a mile. The two silver stud earrings

9

that identified him as a member of the royal guard reflected the sharp sunlight. His breastplate with the curving antlers had clearly been polished for the occasion. "King Callun wants to see you also, Ren. Urgently."

Berin spun his horse around almost before he had finished speaking, his large stature cutting a path through the gathering crowd like a rock splitting a stream. Ren followed on his mare with Hellic alongside him, the two of them exchanging a glance.

Ren wondered if the Skarlan king's early arrival meant he'd get the chance to meet the man and his daughter before his departure. He had never seen them before outside of paintings. Over a hundred years of conflict had kept each ruler on his own side of the border except for in times of war, and this new peace was reluctant, cold and strange.

The courtyard, when they entered, was alive with activity. The main gates flanked by guards were wide open. Guests were arriving, not just from within the city itself, but from all over Frayne, lords and ladies invited to participate in celebrating their future king.

Ren handed the reins of his mare to a stable-boy. A group of servants off-loaded the boar from Niklas' horse and Hellic hovered around it like it was made of glass until he and Ren were ushered inside.

"I'll see you before you leave," Niklas assured Ren, voice raised over the noises of the working crowd as they went their separate ways.

The inside of the castle was, if possible, even more chaotic than the courtyard. Serving girls and slaves flitted around Ren and Hellic in the corridors, muttering pardons and stopping only briefly to offer their crown prince respectful greetings. White and golden ribbons hung from the ceiling and brightly coloured summer flowers brightened the sill of every arched window.

The door to King Callun's private chambers was open. Like Hellic and Ren, Callun didn't seem to be in the best of moods. He paced around the large oak table in the centre of the room, waving away servants arriving with folded sets of clothing as if they were annoying flies. His neatly trimmed beard was shot through with grey hairs and Ren imagined the stress of the Skarlans' arrival had added several new ones.

Hellic greeted Callun as his father, Ren as his king.

"Father, I took down a boar in the woods," Hellic said.

King Callun's smile was strained when he turned towards them and patted Hellic's shoulder. "Really? That's marvellous. Go and change out of your riding clothes. Keelan is waiting for you in your chambers."

Ren looked at Hellic, who lingered, perhaps expecting his father to say more, but the king had already turned his attention to Ren.

Hellic turned and left.

"I'll get ready to depart," Ren said, making to follow Hellic out, but Callun's hand on his shoulder stopped him and turned him back around.

"The transport ship meant to take you has run aground," King Callun said. He looked tired, like he hadn't gotten a good night's sleep in days. "The negotiations have been cancelled."

A rush of joy brought a smile to Ren's face, but the king's expression didn't change, and what he said next made Ren's smile fade as quickly as it had appeared.

"I have another job for you instead. Something important. Return to your rooms and I'll send my advisors to inform you."

"Wait, what?" Ren's jaw went slack, something like absurd laughter bubbling in his stomach. He waited for the king to pat him on the back, wink and tell him to go get ready for the party, but the man's expression remained closed and tired. "I can work tomorrow," Ren argued. "It's Hellic's birthday. The party-"

"I won't argue this, Ren. I'm sorry the circumstances are like this. Now, go."

Ren's brow furrowed, blunt nails digging into his palms. "What… What did I do?"

"Ren, please." The king's voice was tense as he rubbed his brow.

Disappointment settled cold and heavy in Ren's gut. He parted his lips to argue further, but Callun cut him off before he could speak. "Do I have to order you, Ren? I won't say it again."

Ren could hear by Callun's tone that he meant it, so he

swallowed his bitter disappointment and left the chambers, slamming the door behind him.

Perhaps if he hurried, he could finish quickly and might only miss an hour of the celebrations. The Skarlans were early, after all, and the real entertainment wouldn't start until later tonight. It sparked some hope in Ren as he passed the servants and slaves. Dressed in white, they rushed to and from the kitchen and supply rooms with food, wine, cups, and plates. Their feet skidded and slipped against the shining marble floors, but they never lost their balance. They didn't slow down as they passed him, but respectfully nodded their heads. Like the citizens in the streets of Aleria, the staff and courtiers living in the castle treated him as they treated his brothers, a mindset Ren knew had been strictly enforced by the king. Ren, Hellic, and their younger brother Thais were the Stags of Frayne, the pride and future of the country.

Personally, Ren didn't care much for formalities so long as people would come to his bed when he bid them.

Two guards in white and gold armour flanked the doorway to his chambers. The unusual sight made Ren pause before he stepped past them and pushed the door open.

Immediately, his heart sank.

A pile of papers nearly as tall as a child was stacked neatly on his desk next to a vial of ink and a quill.

Paperwork. That was the job? A massive pile of paperwork?

The anger and disappointment that had temporarily settled flared up inside Ren and he kicked the door shut with his heel and marched over to his desk.

"This has got to be a joke," he hissed as he flipped through the top layers of the pile. Not much of it made sense. The papers were lined with rows of numbers and some of it looked like stock, inventory, and trade agreements. Paperwork was a slow, tedious job for bookkeepers and royal advisors, taking place in dusty old libraries. It wasn't a job for the queen's son on the most important day of the year.

Ren lowered the papers and looked around the room, almost expecting someone to jump out from behind his bed or dresser and shout "just kidding!"

A soft click made him turn around, but it wasn't the smiling face of a joker that met him. Instead, the soft and friendly features of Keelan, Hellic's personal slave met him in the doorway.

"Do you need a hand, my lord?" Keelan asked.

For a moment, some of Ren's anger dissipated. Keelan was a sweet boy, and the two of them had always gotten on well. Gifted to Hellic on his thirteenth birthday, Keelan had been everything you could desire in a slave, meek and soft-spoken, with delicate orange curls and a face destined to turn heads with age. But the crown prince had never shown much interest in boys. Ren, on the other hand, had found the young and beautiful slave pleasant and agreeable both as a server, and, when the boy grew old enough, in bed.

"What's with the guards?" Ren asked, gesturing towards the door.

"There are guards outside Hellic's chambers, too. They're everywhere. The staff say it's because of the Skarlans. His Majesty wants to be safe rather than sorry, I suppose," Keelan explained as he closed the distance between them and began loosening the straps of Ren's hunting jacket without being asked. Ren extended his arms to make the job easier.

"I thought you'd be on a ship by now, my lord," Keelan continued.

Ren groaned, extending one leg to let Keelan undo the lacing of his boot and tug it off. "I'm grounded, apparently. I can't leave my room before I'm done with this." He pointed over his shoulder at the pile of papers.

When Keelan lifted his head to look, his eyes went wide and he temporarily forgot about Ren's other boot, leaving him balanced on one leg. "What, really? All of it?"

Ren answered with a shrug, expression sour.

"What made the king so angry with you?" Keelan asked, turning his attention back to tugging off Ren's other boot before placing them both aside.

"I don't know. I can't for the life of me figure out what I did wrong." Tension entered Ren's voice again. "It's as if he's determined to keep me away from this party."

A line formed between Keelan's finely arched eyebrows as he stood, taking Ren's jacket from him when Ren slipped it off his shoulder. "What's at the party that he doesn't want you to see?" Keelan asked, then flushed, realising what kind of dangerous, rebellious thought he had just planted in Ren's head. By then, it was too late.

"Maybe I should find out," Ren said slowly.

Avoiding being spotted by the king would be easy. Keeping out of sight of the guards would be harder. The more he thought it over, though, the more it seemed like an interesting challenge. Perhaps he'd even be able to surprise Hellic. The thought was appealing.

"Are you really sure? It sounds like a bad idea," Keelan said. He looked nervous, hugging Ren's jacket to his chest.

"Don't worry about me," Ren said. He leaned in to press a fleeting kiss to the youth's cheek. "Just don't tell anyone."

CHAPTER TWO

It took Ren almost two hours to get rid of the advisors. They all sat around him, explaining in slow, dry voices what each section meant, what each combination of numbers stood for, and where and how to mark each royal agreement.

Luckily, life at court had taught Ren how to feign interest and act engaged, so he managed to avoid further lengthy explanations that could easily have dragged on all afternoon.

Advisor Selva offered to stay and help him with the second batch, but Ren politely declined, assuring the advisor that he worked best by himself, but appreciated the offer.

Finally, he was alone.

Outside, Ren could hear the muffled sounds of the court and their guests preparing for the luncheon. Ren left his desk and wandered over to the window facing the gardens. Lords and ladies balanced slender cups of welcome drinks between their fingers as they wandered through the gardens. Servants decked the horseshoe-shaped arrangement of tables that ran around the edge of the large outdoor stage. Performers would entertain the guests there as they ate, and after dinner, the stage would be cleared to make space for dancing. In the morning, the lords and ladies feeling fresh enough to ride a horse after the previous night's drunken stupor would be invited out for a morning hunt. Ren didn't need to be there for all of it, just the best parts.

It was clear that the staff had not been prepared for the Skarlans to arrive early enough to partake in lunch. Orders were passed around in tense and clipped voices as servers ran back and forth between the tables and the double doors that led into the castle. Ren smiled to himself. The contained chaos would work to his advantage.

In his dresser, Ren found a white and gold jacket, a pair of fitted trousers, and one of several pairs of new boots he hadn't yet had the chance to wear. Something simple, more in lieu with the guards' uniform that would keep him from sticking out like a sore thumb. With a fine-toothed comb, he brushed his golden hair, still tousled from the hunt, out of his face. A few longer strands fell back down and brushed his cheekbone. He'd have to get Keelan to cut it for him, soon. The boy had more finesse with a pair of scissors than Danali, who had once left Ren with a buzz that had taken weeks to grow back out.

Crossing the room to the opposite window, Ren looked down into the courtyard. At this hour, it was empty – just as he had hoped. Even the guards were busy elsewhere, likely escorting the Skarlan king and his following to the guest rooms under the highest possible amount of supervision.

Carefully, Ren stepped up onto the window sill. He knew where to place his feet and which cracks between the stones would accommodate his fingers. Having one of the chambers closest to the ground had allowed Ren to conduct many secret outings this way – most often to the stables or the stock rooms where he would meet with the sons or daughters of wealthy lords and ladies who wouldn't approve of their heirs sleeping with the queen's bastard son.

Leaning back slightly, Ren let go of the wall and let himself fall the remaining distance to the ground, bending his knees on impact. Landing on stone sent hard shocks up his legs, but all it took to ease the feeling was a light shake of each foot.

Careful to stick close to the walls, Ren followed the edges of the courtyard, slipped through the engraved arches, and passed by the private gardens. The sound of voices grew louder as he neared the main garden and he slowed his pace.

The main garden was a large, airy space, fringed by colonnades that formed open outdoor walkways. Slipping behind one of the broad frescoed pillars, Ren leaned sideways to spy on

19

the guards positioned at precise intervals around the edges of the garden. There were more guards gathered than would usually be at parties, although the Skarlans of course wouldn't know that.

A guest approached the guards nearest Ren and they turned towards her, ready to answer whatever question she had posed. Seeing his chance, Ren had just prepared himself to slip past when a voice stopped him in his tracks.

"What are you doing here? Shouldn't you be in your chambers?"

Containing an exasperated sigh, Ren turned back around. The voice belonged to Thais, the youngest of the three Stags and the king's second true-born son. Unlike his easy relationship with Hellic, Ren had never seemed able to get along with Thais.

"I should, but I'd rather be here. Are you going to tell on me?" Ren asked, angling a challenging look at Thais. Even at sixteen, Thais understood well how to use what little status he had over Ren in any way he could.

Thais shrugged and looked around, taking his time. Every moment he wasted increased the chances of Ren getting caught. Ren wished Thais would just go away.

"Not if you help me out," Thais said finally.

"With what?" Ren asked suspiciously, crossing his arms over his chest, but his cool facade was broken when the two guards returned to their posts, forcing him to wiggle further into the shadow of the pillar.

Thais coughed into the palm of his hand and the sound made Ren look over his shoulder like a cat about to be caught with its paw in the milk. Little shit.

"I just saw some Skarlan guards unload a slave into the castle dungeon," Thais said. "He wore more chains than a raging bull. He looked like a Lowlander. He had their tattoos all over his arm. I asked the guards who he was, but they wouldn't tell me, not even when I told them I was a prince." Thais puckered his lips in a bemused expression. "They were very rude. I want to know why they've brought him here."

Ren narrowed his eyes. "And you want me to go and ask him what he's doing here? Why are you so interested in a Lowlander? They're dangerous – you should mind your own business."

Thais just shrugged. "If you don't do it, I'll tell Father on you."

"You're a little shit," Ren said, voicing his earlier thought aloud.

"So you'll do it?"

"Fine," Ren said, eager to get Thais to stop bothering him so he could escape his precarious hiding place behind the pillar.

* * *

Sneaking into the dungeons was easier than sneaking into the party, but it was the last place Ren wanted to be. He rarely had cause to venture there – in fact, he made a habit of avoiding it at

21

all costs. The dark and clammy atmosphere made his skin crawl. Worst of all, it was the entrance to the lion pit.

Ren could hear the animals growling the moment he reached the bottom step. The corridor was dark and narrow and despite pressing his body against the opposite wall, he couldn't avoid their piercing stares as all three massive cats turned towards him.

They were behind thick iron bars, each chained to a ring in the floor, but their pit was the only cell in the dungeons without a ceiling. Scattered on the ground were the remnants of a carcass the beasts had been feasting on that same morning, their muzzles still stained with blood. When Ren had been younger, he'd had frequent nightmares of the cats scaling the walls and making their way into the castle.

Once Ren was safely past the lions' cell, he could breathe again. Now that he was out of their view, the lions seemed to calm and Ren could focus on locating the cell that held the mysterious prisoner.

All the cells he passed were empty. Ren couldn't remember a time when the dungeons had ever been full. Only the lions were permanent residents in the claustrophobic darkness.

Ren nearly walked straight by him. He sat in the shadows in the corner of his cell, still as a statue and almost invisible, but his head turned just an inch when Ren walked by, and the movement caught Ren's eye. He stopped and turned back towards the cell.

The prisoner was a Lowlander, all right.

From where he sat, he looked almost as ominous as the lions. Ren had never been this close to a Lowlander before. There were some in the city, begging for money in alleys and on street corners, but the guards his family travelled with were always efficient at keeping them at a distance. Ren had heard stories of the Lowlanders since he was a child, some of them perhaps a little too wild to be true. Nursery rhymes and old wives' talk meant to scare children into obedience. Yet, there was no doubt that the Lowlanders were a dangerous kind.

Ren could remember very little actual fact about them from history and geography lessons. A collection of smaller villages in southern Skarlan made up the Lowlands. Instead of purging their lands of the volatile strangers, the Skarlans used them as a resource, as slaves and workers in their capital city of Iskaal. Ren had always thought it seemed like a terrible idea to let them wander around so freely.

"Get up," Ren said, filling his voice with as much authority as he could. He positioned himself very carefully out of arms reach from the bars of the cell.

For a moment, it seemed that the man would ignore his order. Then, slowly, he stood.

"Come forward." Ren's voice echoed in the silence of the dungeons.

When the prisoner took a step into the light, Ren took a step back.

23

The man was no less intimidating in the light.

He was tall, with broad shoulders and a lean but powerful build. His dark hair was pulled back from his face into a short, tufted ponytail.

Ren's eyes travelled down. The Lowlander was shirtless, skin golden, and the tattoo Thais had mentioned covered his right arm from elbow to wrist. But what drew Ren's eye most was the jagged scar that ran vertically from his armpit up over his collarbone to the top of his shoulder. Other, smaller scars criss-crossed his chest and arms, although none as obvious as the one on his shoulder.

Ren hadn't expected him to be handsome, but he noted with a sting of displeasure that the Lowlander was both taller and fitter than himself. Maybe a few years older, too.

Ren huffed. "What's your name, prisoner?"

The silence stretched on. The young man's entire body was tense, as if he expected Ren to lash out at him at any moment. The look in his eyes was pure and unshielded hatred, the intensity of it forcing Ren to avert his gaze.

"Anik," the Lowlander replied finally.

"What are you doing here, prisoner?" Ren continued, keeping his voice carefully level.

"I don't know," the prisoner – Anik – responded, his words coloured by a slight, flowing accent that Ren found surprisingly pleasant. It turned his voice softer than Ren thought it would be.

Ren pushed the thought aside, setting his jaw. "Don't lie to me," he demanded.

"I don't know," Anik repeated in the same tone, angling his chin up with a jerk. "Skahli."

Frowning at the unfamiliar word, Ren's eyes settled on the tattoos on the Lowlander's arm. He needed at least something interesting to tell Thais so Thais wouldn't rat him out. Time was passing quickly; lunch would be served at any moment. "What's that about?" he asked, pointing to the black markings.

Slowly, Anik touched the top part of the tattoo with the tips of two fingers. It looked like curving antlers circling his forearm. "This? My first kill was a stag," he said, and met Ren's eyes.

Ren swallowed involuntarily. The Lowlander's first kill was the symbol of Frayne's royal family. Of himself, Hellic and Thais. A coincidence? It had to be. This man had probably never set foot in Frayne before in his life. The prisoner was simply trying to scare him. He certainly seemed to have enough contained anger to confirm all the stories about the Lowlanders Ren had heard, and Ren wasn't interested in staying one moment longer. However little he had managed to drag from the eerie Lowlander, it'd have to be enough.

Stepping back from the iron bars of the cell, Ren didn't turn around until he was out of sight and then some. He made his way swiftly past the lion pit, although he still startled when one of the giant beasts shifted, disturbed by the sound of his footsteps, its

25

piercing yellow eyes boring into his.

Ren was so focused on looking over his shoulder that the impact of a body against his own nearly made him jump out of his skin. But the figure in front of him was a person, not a beast. And not just any person.

Although Ren had never seen King Halvard up close, he was unmistakable. He was a large man, with broad shoulders, a trimmed beard, and a thick fur cloak wrapped around his shoulders despite the mild weather. Around his neck hung a golden chain, the links nearly as thick as a baby's wrist.

"Excuse me, Your Majesty," Ren said quickly, bowing his head. He made to move past the king, but stopped when a second man stepped up alongside him and blocked Ren's path. This man was considerably leaner, but radiated just as much authority. Ren had heard of King Halvard's first advisor, the cold and unsettling Lord Nathair. None of the stories had been pleasant.

"What's your name, boy?" King Halvard asked, narrowing his blue eyes.

Ren looked between the two men, unable to shake the feeling of being out of his depth. He kept his eyes respectfully lowered. "Ren, Your Majesty."

The king's face turned red, and without warning, he reached out and grabbed Ren by the front of the shirt. "Ren Frayne? The late queen's bastard son?"

Startled, Ren closed a hand around the king's wrist and tried to pull away, but the man's grip was like iron. "Y-yes. I didn't mean to disturb your prisoner, Your Majesty," Ren assured him.

King Halvard suddenly let go and Ren took a few steps back. The look the king sent his advisor was one full of outrage. Despite that, Lord Nathair smiled, although it looked more like the expression a fox would have right before entering a hen house.

Ren swallowed. Thais owed him more than silence for this.

"You're free to disturb him all you wish, Lord Ren. He's for you," Nathair said.

Ren blinked. "For me?" he asked, bemused. He glanced at the king, but the man's expression was unreadable. How could the prisoner be for him if he wasn't even supposed to be here? It had to be a mistake. "I think you might be-" Ren started, but Nathair cut him off.

"He's all yours. For your enjoyment."

Ren shook his head. His plan to sneak into the party was already at risk. Accepting a gift from the king of Skarlan would definitely get him exposed.

"I'm sorry, I don't want... He's not-"

"No matter," Nathair interrupted, shining Ren another fox-like smile. "He's yours now, so you can do with him as you please. Or are you going to refuse the gift of a king? He was not cheap, nor easy to tame."

Ren looked from Nathair to King Halvard, who still hadn't

spoken. At Nathair's words, the king seemed to shake himself out and gave a firm nod.

"It's a fine gift. You'd do well not to refuse, boy," King Halvard said.

Ren bowed deeply. "Very well. Thank you, Your Majesty," Ren said slowly. As he watched, Lord Nathair placed a hand against the king's chest and physically pushed him aside so Ren could pass. When Ren did, he dared one last glance at the king. He was pale, body stiff.

Ren left the dungeons as fast as he could, relieved to breathe in the fresh air above ground.

However he had imagined King Halvard, this certainly hadn't been it.

* * *

"So?" Thais asked, ambushing Ren as soon as he left the courtyard.

"You were right," Ren said, glancing around. "It's a Lowlander. His name is Anik and he got one of his tattoos from killing a stag when he was a kid or something. Good enough?"

"That's it?" Thais asked, upper lip curling in disdain. "That's all you found out?"

"Are you going to be quiet or not?"

"Fine." Thais sighed and brushed his brown locks back from

28

his eyes. "Father and Hellic still haven't arrived. I don't know what's taking them so long. I think the guests are starting to get impatient."

Thais followed Ren as he sneaked around the side of one of the pale sandstone walls. Leaning around the corner, Ren watched as a lady of the court engaged with a particularly handsome guard. As soon as the guard turned his back, Ren slipped past and into the garden. So long as he stayed in the crowd, he likely wouldn't be spotted. Behind Ren, Thais strolled through the pale arches. Now that he had gotten what he wanted from Ren, he seemed content to leave him be, instead drifting towards the tables decked with bowls of grapes and honey-covered pear.

It didn't take long for the guests, lords and ladies both, to start gravitating to Ren. The three golden stud earrings in his left ear advertised him as a prince, even to people who had never met him before. Being a bastard meant he wasn't really entitled to all three of them, but his mother and King Callun had always gone out of their way to treat all their sons equally. Ren was a Stag, like Hellic and Thais.

Sauntering over to the serving tables, Ren scooped up a golden goblet of red wine as he scanned the crowd. This was where he found himself most comfortable: in the midst of the game of giving and seeking information, soaking up everything valuable. Ren had perfected the ability to sound deeply interested in each and every person's gossip. People like these enjoyed feeling like they were friends with royalty, and it was surprising how much people were willing to share when faced with a prince's caring and empathetic smile. More than once, it had resulted in good deals. The prize mare with the silken steel grey coat Ren had gifted to Hellic on his fifteenth birthday had only cost Ren a single night under the rolling body of a nameless duke Ren had never seen again, but who was well known for his excellent steeds and would absolutely not sell his stunning yearling filly for any price. At least, not until Ren had shed his undershirt and made the duke forget all about his previous statements.

"Lord Ren! Oh, look how you've grown. The last time I saw you, you were no taller than this."

Ren turned to see a lord with blond hair and a hooked nose wiggling a hand at waist height as he approached, a wine glass dangling precariously from the fingers of his other hand.

Ren looked around to make sure none of the guards had heard his name mentioned, then turned a brilliant smile on the man. "Lord Aevis. It's wonderful to see you again," Ren said, shaking the man's hand.

"I was so sorry to hear about your grandfather. I heard his passing wasn't a peaceful one," Lord Aevis said, offering Ren one of the doe-eyed expressions Ren himself had long since perfected.

"Thank you, Lord Aevis. It was a difficult time and we're all still grieving," Ren said, letting his voice go faintly rough. "If there's anything at all I can do for you, let me know. Losing loved ones isn't easy."

"It really isn't," Ren agreed, shaking both of Lord Aevis' hands again. "Thank you so much. You're very kind."

"So, where is your brother?" Lord Aevis looked around, head whipping back and forth in a way that reminded Ren of a watchful ferret. "I'd like to greet the birthday boy before the meal begins."

"I think he's still getting ready, I'm afraid. I'll ask for him," Ren said, smiling again as he slipped past Lord Aevis.

He looked around. By the central fountain stood a young man in a maroon and golden formal jacket, engaged in quiet conversation with an older lady. Ren narrowed his eyes, trying to place the man's face. Lord Alasander perhaps? Brother of Lord Elgrin, the ruler of Draxia in the south. Now that Ren thought of it, it was unusual for Lord Elgrin not to make an appearance. Perhaps something had come up, forcing him to send his brother in his place. Either way, it was of little use to Ren.

Lady Cavazé over by the roses, however, had recently acquired seven brand new warships for the protection of her fort by the sea. Chatting her up might prove fruitful. Last time they'd met, she had seemed particularly interested in what was underneath Ren's form-fitting jacket. Maybe it was time to let her have a peek. Ren's father might have been a lowly slave, but at

31

least the man's poor blood had allowed Ren to inherit all of his mother's good looks, his greatest resource in a place such as this.

He was about to approach Lady Cavazé when a heavy hand fell on his shoulder.

The last person Ren expected to see when he turned around was King Halvard. At least this time, the king seemed to have collected himself. He smiled pleasantly at Ren. "Your brother and the king are taking their time. Why don't we bring out some entertainment while we wait?"

It was a rhetorical question, and the king didn't wait for Ren to answer. Instead, he lifted a hand above the crowd to get the attention of the staff. "Let's have Prince Ren's new slave perform," he boomed. To Ren, he said, "I think you'll change your mind about him. He's talented. Come, let us all be seated."

Ren grit his teeth. There was no way the guards wouldn't have overheard the king's loud declaration, and when Ren looked around, he saw at least five of them turn to stare directly at him, and then at each other. Slowly, it dawned on him that they weren't going to act and risk causing a scene in front of the Skarlan king. A slow smile spread across Ren's face.

Ren took a seat at the centre table next to Thais. From across the gardens, Ren caught a glimpse of Berin, and the look of surprise and worry on the man's face almost made Ren feel a sting of guilt. Berin was one of the best men he knew, and he didn't deserve King Callun's wrath for letting Ren slip past his guards. Maybe Ren could talk to the king about it later.

As the remaining courtiers and guests settled themselves at the table, King Halvard gestured for the slave to be brought out.

At Halvard's other side sat his daughter, Princess Evalyne. Leaning forward, Ren assessed her. Hellic might be pleased to find that she was unusually beautiful. She sat with her head bowed and looked at her empty plate, her fiery hair falling in soft waves over one shoulder.

On the other side of Thais, the centre seats that belonged to Hellic and King Callun remained glaringly empty, so Keelan positioned himself behind Ren's chair instead.

Leaning back in his seat, Ren couldn't help a slight feeling of unease. It wasn't like Hellic and the king to leave such important guests waiting.

"Keelan," Ren said softly over his shoulder. "Will you get someone to go check on my brother and the king? The meal is about to start."

Keelan nodded and disappeared into the castle behind them, and Ren turned his attention back to the stage.

From beneath one of the arches that led to the courtyard came the prisoner, Anik, flanked by a pair of guards. He was unchained, and in his hands were three knives. Ren raised his eyebrows. Despite Anik being a Lowlander, the king didn't seem overly concerned about the slave wielding so many sharp weapons. More than likely, they'd been dulled, but a thrown knife

33

could still take an eye.

The entire crowd went silent as Anik took centre stage. He was still shirtless and barefoot, although the tattered trousers he'd worn in the cell had been replaced by plain black ones.

Ren glanced at the guests seated at the horseshoe-shaped arrangement of tables around him. Some of them regarded Anik with the same displeasure you would a ham left too long in the summer heat. Others, to Ren's surprise, looked in his direction with frowns and tight lips as if they blamed him for bringing a pet pig to a fine dinner. Ren narrowed his eyes at them. He wasn't the one who had made the suggestion to have the prisoner perform. A petty part of him hoped the sight of the unwashed Lowlander would make them lose their appetites.

Anik tossed all three knives high into the air, spun around, and caught all three by the handles. Without a moment's pause, he flowed into a dangerously fast juggling act. The crowd oohed and ahhed at the sight, seeming to momentarily forget their disdain, but Ren found himself less than impressed. The slave the king had gifted him was a jester? Not particularly useful. And unless Ren ever needed to know how to skin a squirrel or navigate by the stars, he would have no use for the cranky Lowlander. Maybe he could put him to work in the stables.

The low hum of voices to Ren's right turned louder and more insistent. Ren turned his head to see Lord Nathair not watching the performance, but speaking firmly with a pair of guards. Ren couldn't hear what he said, but his gaze was intense. Suddenly, Nathair stood and pointed to the Lowlander. "Stop him!" Nathair's sharp voice cut through the mumbling of the guests and silence fell. People looked around, confused.

Ren watched, brow furrowing, as Nathair stepped around the tables and marched onto the sand of the stage. "Apprehend him," he commanded.

Two Skarlan guards moved quickly, crossing the distance to Anik and taking hold of his wrists, prying the knives from his hands before twisting his arms behind his back. At the high table, the king sat stone-faced. Had Halvard gone back on his decision to gift Ren the slave? That suited Ren just fine. Or maybe he had just been ridiculously slow to notice the fact that the man was tossing sharp objects around in close proximity to royalty. The thought amused Ren.

Nathair approached Anik and the Lowlander tried to backtrack, feet finding no purchase against the sand with a guard's firm grip around each of his arms. When Nathair reached for him, Anik twisted his body to the side, but that only made it easier for Nathair to grab what was tucked under the waistband of the Lowlander's trousers.

What Nathair held high in the air for the entire crowd to see shone in the sunlight: the blade of a knife covered in fresh blood.

The garden was dead silent and Nathair's voice carried to every corner of it. "Prince Ren's slave seems to have been up to no good."

Several faces turned towards Ren, who froze with his cup of wine halfway to his lips, heat rising to his face against his will.

"What have you done, slave?" Nathair asked, turning back towards the Lowlander, who was breathing heavily, as if he couldn't get enough air into his lungs. Not a word left his mouth.

Then Nathair turned to look at Ren, his steel-grey eyes boring into Ren's. "Care to explain this?"

Ren blinked. Everyone was watching him now, even the servants. Ren's mouth felt dry. A part of him hoped this was part of the performance, that it would all end in laughs and jokes, but the more reasonable side of him knew that it wasn't. When he spoke, his voice seemed too loud in the silence. "Explain what?"

"The slave is yours," Nathair said, spreading his arms out to the side. "He does what he is ordered to do. Didn't the king and I meet you in the dungeons on your way up from the slave's cell? What were you doing there?"

Ren's lips parted. Anik hadn't even belonged to him at that point. He was about to argue when the doors leading into the castle flew open and Keelan stumbled out, face white as a sheet.

"The king," Keelan gasped, his entire body shaking. "The king and the crown prince are dead."

CHAPTER THREE

The first thing Ren saw was the blood, too stark and bright against the shining beige-and-gold floors of the corridor. He had been the first inside, racing through the audience chamber and down the hall with his heart in his throat, beating so fast he thought he'd choke on it. He pushed through the gathered crowd of slaves and servants and froze in his tracks.

Even as he saw them, he couldn't stop desperately wishing it wasn't true.

Hellic's eyes were open, staring without seeing the gold filigreed ceiling. His throat was slit, a deep, grim gash all the way across, his fine white formal jacket with the golden antlers around the collar stained red.

King Callun lay a few feet away, face-down on the cold, hard floor, stabbed in the back just inside the doorway to his chambers. The blood still spread in a growing pool, thick and dark. The scent of it was heavy on the air.

Ren's vision narrowed. The world was spinning. The air seemed too thin to breathe. The impact of his knees against the floor echoed, but he didn't feel it.

"Hellic," he called, barely recognizing the sound of his own voice, hoarse and hysterical. His chest ached as if the knife that had butchered his baby brother was now buried between his ribs, twisting slowly. "Hellic! Someone help him."

Ren reached out. Hands closed around his biceps to help him to his feet, but he struggled against them.

"No, Hellic, please…"

He needed to be with his brother, needed to help him. The hands tightened.

"Lock him in his chambers. Position two guards at the door."

The hands weren't trying to help him at all.

Twisting around, Ren met the stony face and cold eyes of Lord Nathair.

"What are you doing?" Ren gasped. His mind felt fractured. The world around him was awash with confusion.

"You stand accused of the murder of the king and the crown prince of Frayne. Take him away," Nathair said, giving his order to the Skarlan guards that held Ren. Around them, Fraynean guards looked on in shock, but did nothing to oppose the king's word.

They dragged Ren away, his feet skidding along the floor, past guards in white and gold frantically trying to keep guests and courtiers at bay.

They couldn't do this. This was his family.

Behind him, Ren heard Thais' broken voice calling out for his father.

* * *

The sudden silence when the door to his chambers was shut and locked was deafening. Ren stood in the middle of his bedroom where the guards had left him and stared at the door.

The world swayed. Turning, he managed to stagger over to the empty water basin before his insides cramped and his stomach emptied itself. Bile burned in his throat. The breaths he drew in were rasping and his muscles clenched as he retched again.

His next ragged breath ended in a sob as he sank into the chair at his desk, his grip on the wooden edge white-knuckled.

Hellic was dead. King Callun was dead.

Ren's breaths came fast now and he dropped his head onto the hard wooden desk as the edges of his vision turned dark.

Hellic was dead.

The king was dead.

Ren stared at the lines and patterns of the wood in front of his face until he thought he was no longer on the verge of blacking out. He wasn't sure how long he sat there, staring numbly ahead.

Bells were ringing. Loud and slow, they announced the tragedy across the city.

They couldn't really think he was a killer, could they? He had barely spent five minutes in the dungeon before the Skarlan king and his advisor had shown up.

The Skarlan king.

Realisation hit Ren like the kick of a horse and he sat up straight, feeling the need to vomit again, although his stomach was painfully empty.

He hadn't realised it at first, shock and horror drowning out everything else, but now the truth opened itself up to him like the maw of a vile creature.

Skarlan and Frayne had been at war for generations. King Halvard had strolled right into the heart of Frayne under the false pretence of an unstable peace agreement and killed the king and the crown prince. Halvard had brought the slave, had set Ren up and accused him of murder. The entire royal family wiped out with a single blow. All except for Thais, too young to rule alone. How had no one seen it? This was grounds for war. They should be apprehending Halvard and his entourage and throwing them all in the dungeon.

Ren's eyes narrowed. The only thing that didn't fit was himself. He was never supposed to have been at the party, and judging by Halvard's reaction when Ren had bumped into him in the dungeons, he hadn't expected to see Ren there either. Something like this must have required planning. It didn't add up.

Ren thought about King Callun looking stressed and tired in his chambers before the party. He had been so adamant that Ren should stay away. The horrible thought that Callun had known this was going to happen crossed his mind, but he violently brushed it aside. If Callun had known about Halvard's plans, he would have defended himself, defended Hellic. He would never have even let Halvard inside.

Going over to the window on stiff, clumsy legs, Ren leaned against the frame. Fraynean guards were stationed all around the courtyard. They stood uneasily, glancing at each other and talking to their partners. Whose command were they under? What was happening now? Golden ribbons still decorated the inner walls of the courtyard like a cruel kind of mockery. Ren turned his face away.

Thais, as Hellic's true-born younger brother, was currently the highest authority in the castle. Where was he? Where was Berin, the captain of the guard?

Going over to the door, Ren wiggled the handle and then pounded a fist against the wood. "Hey! Open the door. I need to talk to the captain. It's important."

The other side remained silent. Ren knew Nathair had ordered two guards stationed at his door, but regardless of whether they

41

were Fraynean or Skarlan, they clearly weren't going to take orders from him.

With a frustrated groan, he strode over to the garden-side window. There had to be a way out. He had to figure out what was going on. The king was dead and the country's greatest rival was within castle walls. Frayne had never before been in this much danger.

"Fuck," Ren hissed, slamming his hand against the window sill. Tears welled in his eyes again, but he blinked them away furiously. The gardens were guarded too, by just two men, but they were both facing his way.

Hours passed. Three times, Ren banged on the door. All three times, he got only silence in response. He opened the window and shouted to the guards, but they didn't even look at him. If Thais was in charge, why didn't he order Ren released? Unless Thais wasn't in charge at all. Or worse yet, if he really believed Ren was behind the murder. Nathair had planted the seed of Ren's guilt when he had raised the slave's knife in the air for the entire court to see.

Hours passed. Darkness fell and no one came for him, not even to deliver food. Ren lay on his back on the bed, but he was wide awake. He hadn't eaten since that morning, but food was the last thing on his mind. Each time he closed his eyes for more than a second, he saw blood. Hellic's dead eyes staring up at the ceiling. The gash in his brother's throat. Without warning, tears welled up in his eyes and kept threatening to spill. He'd never sleep again for the rest of his life.

Instead, Ren spent the dark hours thinking about Thais, Niklas, Berin, and Keelan. The royal slaves: kind-hearted Danali who had served the king and demure Avery who was supposed to be a calming influence on Thais, but who had never really caught the rowdy young prince's attention. What would happen to them now? Were they safe? Or were they already dead, their throats slit like Hellic's? More than anything, Ren wished he could turn back time. To that morning, when Hellic had been alive and they had both been happy. Happy and safe.

The next time Ren closed his eyes, he saw a throne room littered with bodies and King Halvard on his family's throne.

A muffled tapping sound disturbed his thoughts and he sat up, eyes wide in the darkness. Fingers fumbling, he lit a candle and carried it with him, tracking the sound to the window facing the courtyard.

Ren could have wept at the sight of a familiar face.

Putting the candle down, Ren quickly pushed the window open and Niklas gripped the frame. He was balancing on the narrow ledge made by the frame of the window below.

"We don't have much time." Niklas' voice was a tense whisper. His light brown hair was ruffled from sleep. "Berin sent the guards for rounds, but they'll be back in a few minutes. Halvard's men are watching everything."

Below, Ren could just about make out Berin's large form in the darkness.

"What's happening?" Ren whispered. "Where's Thais?"

"Thais was in shock after…what happened," Niklas explained, averting his gaze. "Halvard said he wanted to take care of him. He took him to the inner chambers. He won't let anyone in and Berin is afraid to do anything in case they try to use Thais as a hostage. Halvard knows Thais is the only heir Frayne has left, so everyone's hands are tied."

"What is he planning?" Ren asked. "What's going to happen now?"

Niklas looked over his shoulder at Berin. When he answered, his voice was dark. "Halvard wants to execute you and the slave for murder at dawn tomorrow."

Ren's heart skipped a beat. It had already been dark for hours. Dawn wasn't far away. "But he can't do that, can he? People don't really think I did it, right?"

Niklas' expression was tortured. "It doesn't matter. Don't you understand, Ren? The king is dead. Halvard has Thais. He can do whatever he wants and blame whomever he wants."

"But why? Killing me won't make a difference. Killing Thais won't make Halvard king of Frayne. He can't keep Thais hostage in the inner chambers forever." Ren's voice trembled.

"Niklas," Berin called quietly.

"We're out of time," Niklas said, offering Ren an apologetic expression as he reached out to squeeze his hand.

"I need to get out of here," Ren said, swallowing against the returning feeling of nausea.

Niklas nodded. "We're working on it. Berin's going to find a way to get the guards away from the courtyard and the battlements. Be ready before dawn. We'll come get you."

"But where do I go?" Ren asked, panic rising inside him.

Niklas was already climbing back down the wall.

"I'm sorry, Ren. I have to go – someone will notice if we're gone too long. Be ready before dawn," Niklas whispered as loudly as he could before he and Berin slipped away into the shadows. In the very next second, the guards returned from their rounds.

* * *

Time had never before passed so slowly.

Hours before dawn, Ren was ready to go. He filled his travel bag with clothes, a pair of extra boots, and a knife, and put on his dark hunting jacket with the deep hood that would help conceal his appearance.

Opening his desk drawer, he pushed aside notes and papers before finding what he was searching for at the bottom.

He drew out the small filigree key, closing his hand around it with a new ache in his chest.

45

His mother had given him that key only a few days before she died.

Closing the drawer, Ren sat down on the edge of his bed, fingertips tracing the delicate metal swirls. It calmed him.

He could remember the day she had given it to him, the two of them sitting with their legs drawn up on her bed, the infant Thais, only a day old, asleep in a crib by the window. "For when you need to escape," she had said, pressing the key against his palm. Her eyes had been wide, brow furrowed by a worry Ren hadn't understood then – and still didn't.

Six years old, he had run up and down the hallways of the castle and tried the key in all the locks, but it hadn't fit any of them. After that, he had tried the stables, the barracks, even the city gates, but to no avail. Three days later, his mother, the queen, was dead and Ren had tossed the key into the drawer. A key meant for escape was no use if it didn't work on any doors.

Flipping the key over, he closed his hand around it. He needed to escape now. He slipped the key into his pocket.

There was nothing else in the the chambers he could take with him. The carved wooden horse figurine Hellic had made him when they were both children stood atop the dresser. Ren didn't know much about art, but the colourful painting of foxes playing at the foot of a massive tree that hung above his desk had always appealed to him. His collection of finely engraved gold medallions sat in the delicate glass cabinet mounted on the wall, proudly on display. None of those things would be of any use to him on the road. He could only hope they'd still be here waiting for him when he returned.

If he returned.

The small voice in the back of his mind was an unwelcome intrusion and he forcefully purged it from his thoughts.

Ren sank down onto the edge of his bed with a heavy sigh, but a tapping on the window made him jump back onto his feet, his travel bag in hand. Pushing the window open, he looked down and saw Niklas step back from the window, dropping a pebble.

"We have ten minutes," Berin called from behind Niklas. "I called for a guard shift."

Normally, changes of the guard were carried out smoothly, with no holes in the defences, but the Fraynean soldiers had worked under Berin for years, some of them almost as long as Ren had been alive. Ren didn't doubt they'd risk Halvard's wrath if Berin asked them to. Ren just had to make sure it wasn't for naught.

Tossing his bag to Niklas, Ren looked over his shoulder. He was leaving his home behind and had no idea when he would be back. The thought that he might never return filled him with ice-cold fear. Then he pushed that fear aside and swung his legs over the window sill, climbing down to the cobblestones of the courtyard.

"Ride to Teu," Berin instructed, urging Ren around the

perimeter of the courtyard while keeping a close eye on the windows above. "Wait in the inn until nightfall. We'll find a way to sneak out and meet you there. Then we can talk about what to do next."

"Any news about Thais?" Ren asked, but Berin shook his head.

"Take the slave with you."

Ren gawked. "Why?"

"Do you know how to navigate by the stars? Have you ever had to ride anywhere alone that wasn't either the forest or within the city walls?"

Ren hesitated.

"Plus," Berin continued."He's a warrior. You're not. That might prove useful."

"You don't know if-"

"Ren."

"Fine," Ren said, surrendering with a sigh. Maybe Berin's idea wasn't all bad. That was, if the Lowlander didn't decide to kill him before they even made it to Teu.

"Good luck, son. I'll see you tonight," Berin said, giving Ren's shoulders a tight squeeze. Then he was gone. Ren watched him disappear beneath the arches, then turned on his heel and made for the dungeons.

"Where are you going?" Niklas asked, catching up to him with running steps.

"I'm taking the slave with me."

"What? You mean the slave that killed your family?"

Ren grabbed a torch from a sconce, leading the way down the narrow steps to the dungeon. "I don't think he did. And Berin is right, there's a good chance I'll need his help," he said, pointing to the hook on the wall. "Grab the keys."

Niklas murmured something about it being a bad idea, but took the key bundle from the hook on the wall and tossed it to Ren.

"Keep watch by the stairs," Ren instructed.

For the second time in the span of a day, Ren made his way into the dungeons.. Ten minutes. He had to be swift. Hopefully, they hadn't moved Anik to a different part of the castle.

He ran past the lions this time, making them startle and growl in the darkness. Not being able to see them didn't make Ren's heart skip any less. To his relief, Anik was where Ren had hoped he'd be.

"Get up," Ren said, coming to a stop in front of the Lowlander's cell.

The slave was an unmoving figure in the corner, curled up like a cat.

"I said, get up, slave."

The slave lifted his head, but otherwise didn't move. "I told you, my name is Anik. And I don't have to do what you say. I'll be dead in an hour anyway."

Ren banged his hands hard against the metal bars, making them rattle. "I'm fleeing the castle, and you're my slave. You can either sit here and wait to die or come with me," Ren hissed, looking over his shoulder towards the stairs. They were wasting time.

Finally, Anik stirred. Pushing himself upright, he stalked closer to the bars. There was a strange look in his eyes, one Ren couldn't decipher. He looked Ren up and down as if trying to decide whether Ren was playing a trick. "Where are we going?"

"Away from here," Ren said simply, and stuck the key in the lock. The cell door squeaked when it swung open and Ren didn't wait to see if Anik followed him, but turned and ran back towards the stairs where Niklas waited.

Anik stopped behind them. Niklas looked at the tall Lowlander with wide eyes, but said nothing.

"All right, go to the stables," Niklas said, tearing his gaze from Anik. "Keelan is waiting for you." He gripped Ren's wrist before stepping in close and wrapping both arms around him in a tight embrace. "Be careful, Ren. Promise me. I don't want to lose you."

Ren clenched his jaw, leaning into the hug and allowing himself to soak up the comfort it provided. "You, too."

Reaching the stables meant crossing into the open. They ran the distance, Ren's heart in his throat, but no guards called out for them to halt, and they slipped through the stable doors undetected.

"Over here," a hushed voice called. Keelan came towards them a moment later, dragging two horses, one set of reins in each hand. "Berin told me you were bringing the slave. I took our fastest horses, my lord." He handed the reins to Ren and glanced at Anik.

"Thank you, Keelan," Ren said, passing the reins of one horse to Anik before securing his bag to the saddle of the other. He tried not to think about how the contents of that bag was all he had left in the world. He mounted his horse, the grey mare. She was built for speed an endurance, a fine breed.

"Hold on," Keelan said. He handed Ren a saddle bag. "I packed food and water. It should be plenty." His voice trembled.

"You're the best." Ren reached down to give Keelan's shoulder a comforting squeeze, but it only seemed to make the youth tremble worse.

"Can I come with you? Please?" Keelan begged, looking up at Ren with wide, shining eyes. "I'm scared. They killed Danali and Avery and most of the castle slaves."

Tightness constricted Ren's chest. Looking over his shoulder, he gestured for Anik to ride out. The Lowlander didn't seem to need telling twice, and rode his horse right out of the stables and towards the front gates.

Ren's heart ached as he looked back down at Keelan. "Berin will keep you safe. Tell him that's an order. I need you to stay here and watch over Thais. Can you do that for me?" Ren asked.

Keelan's fingers were tight around his wrist. The slave nodded, visibly holding himself together, jaw tight. "You can count on me."

Bending down, Ren pressed a soft kiss to the corner of the Keelan's mouth and nudged his horse forward, wrapping the strap of the extra saddle bag around his wrist.

The gelding's hooves clattered against the cobblestones of the courtyard as he galloped towards the single rider at the gates. As Ren passed between the gateposts, his stomach flipped and he yanked his horse to a stop and turned, looking back at the beautiful sandstone castle with its golden spires, towers, and arches, the white and gold flags billowing in the breeze. It felt like a dream. A grotesque, awful dream of the kind where the mind made up its own worst version of his biggest fears.

"What are you waiting for?" Anik's voice dragged Ren's gaze away from his former home and he turned his horse back around and urged it forward.

* * *

Around them, the first hints of daylight coloured the sky a dull, washed-out grey. Lights from distant buildings dotted the horizon as the citizens of Frayne slowly roused from sleep, unaware of the night's gruesome events.

They made it a mile out of the city before Anik pulled his horse in front of Ren's and forced him to a stop. Ren's gelding skipped backwards, tossing its head.

"It's time you tell me where we're going," Anik said.

"We're heading to Teu. It's a small trading town a day's ride from here. Get out of my way," Ren said, trying to nudge his horse forward. Anik didn't budge.

"They'll chase us down."

"I know."

"Do you even have a plan?" Anik pushed.

"We don't have time to argue," Ren said, leaning forward to snatch the reins of Anik's horse, but Anik swiftly moved the mare sideways and out of Ren's range. Anik's grip was loose on his reins, but the horse seemed attentive to his every command. So he could ride a horse and juggle knives. Ren still wasn't impressed.

"Excuse me if I don't want to die," Anik persisted.

Ren sighed, struggling to push down the frustration rising inside him. Lowlanders really made terrible slaves. When he spoke, his voice was hard. "I don't care what you want and don't want. You're my slave and you have to do what I say."

Anik's expression hardened. His entire body stiffened. He looked like he was seconds from punching Ren in the face and Ren instinctively tensed.

"Move," Ren said again.

Anik's jaw worked, but he turned his horse back alongside Ren's.

"Because you saved my life, I'll follow you to Teu and no further, skahli," Anik said, and nudged his horse into a trot without waiting for Ren.

"That's 'Prince Ren' to you," Ren shouted, hurrying after him.

* * *

A slow-moving river wound its way through the small country town of Teu, with snow-capped mountains as a backdrop against the blue sky. It was a wealthy little town, benefiting from being so close to Frayne's capital city of Aleria, with countless large houses and several fields full of fat cows and fluffy sheep.

A herd of goats crossed their path as Ren and Anik rode into the town. Ren pulled up the hood of his jacket. This close to Aleria, the danger of getting recognized was high, even if no one here yet knew what had transpired in the capital and people weren't on the lookout for a runaway bastard prince. It was better to be safe than sorry. The people they passed barely spared them a glance. Travellers came through here often, going to and from the capital.

The sun touched down on the peak of a far mountain as they tied their horses in front of the inn and went inside. None of the patrons took any note of them as they stepped up to the counter, but Ren still ordered dinner up to their room as he paid for their beds for the night.

Anik hadn't spoken a single word to him since their confrontation on the road. When the innkeeper passed Ren the key, Anik pointed to the map that hung on the wall next to the window. "How much for that?"

The innkeeper looked Anik up and down, taking in his appearance for the first time with a hint of wariness in his gaze. It wasn't hard to guess why. Anik's Lowlander accent was slight but distinct. Glancing over his shoulder, Ren saw several of the inn guests watching them now, and he quickly turned his face away.

The innkeeper shook his head. "It's not for sale."

"Five gold?"

"No."

"Fifteen?" Anik pressed.

"Anik!" Ren hissed, before Anik could throw any more of his gold at a map.

"Fine." The innkeeper shrugged and went over to take the map off the wall and roll it up. He handed it to Anik. Ren glared at him, but Anik either didn't notice or didn't care.

"Fifteen gold for a map? Are you out of your mind?" Ren asked as they ascended the narrow stairs and let themselves into their room, Ren turning the key in the lock behind them. The room was mostly bare, with two beds, a shared night stand and a small fireplace in the corner.

"You're a prince; you can afford it," Anik said, unrolling the map on the floor without sparing Ren a second glance. He settled there, with his legs folded under him.

"I didn't bring an unlimited amount of money with me, just so you know," Ren said, dropping his bags on the bed closest to the door. His bones and muscles ached even though the ride to Teu had only taken half a day.

"I don't know about you, but I'd prefer to know where I'm going," Anik said without lifting his gaze from the map. Long strands of dark hair fell over the side of his face, hiding his expression from Ren. He walked his fingers across the surface of the map, measuring distances.

Ren paused. Anik had said he would follow Ren to Teu and no further. It occurred to Ren that this was probably Anik's first time in Frayne. He knew the terrain just as little as Ren did. He needed the map to find his way back to the Lowlands, or wherever he planned on going. However, Ren still needed his help. He would simply have to talk Anik out of leaving. At least talking was something Ren knew how to do. Besides, Anik had bought the map with Ren's gold, so technically, it was his.

Kneeling on the bed, Ren dug his hands into the bags and looked over the food Keelan had packed, trying to gauge how long it would last them. It definitely wasn't roast beef and gravy. Keelan had likely taken it from the servants' food storage in the rush. Pushing aside two loaves of bread, Ren paused. There was a scrap of paper at the bottom of the bag, and when he picked it up and turned it over, he instantly recognized Keelan's tiny, curling handwriting.

Stay strong and stay safe.
I know you can do this.
If we don't see each other again, know that I enjoyed every
second in your service.
Keelan.

Ren stared at the note, biting his tongue until the blurriness obscuring his vision went away. There was no way he was going to cry in front of Anik.

Ren glanced at him over his shoulder. There was still something he hadn't considered. His plan had only gone as far as this: the meeting with Berin and Niklas in Teu. But what came after that? The question seemed impossibly huge and heavy, and Ren sank down onto the bed and rubbed both hands over his face.

He wouldn't be able to go home for a long time. The reality remained that the Skarlan king would hold the capital of Frayne until someone found a way to remove him.

What else could Ren do? Run? Leave the country? And then what – live out the rest of his days in some faraway land where no one knew his name, surviving from day to day without family or friends?

Nausea threatened to overcome him once more, and when he stood up to let in some fresh air, the whole world spun around him. He braced a hand against the wall, arms shaking.

"You look like you're about to pass out."

Anik's condescending voice was starting to grate on Ren's nerves, his tone hard and uncaring, as if he'd speak with the same kind of indifference if he was watching Ren being eaten alive by lions.

"I'm going to bathe," Ren said, cringing at the roughness of his own voice. The bath had been on the list of services this inn offered, which was apparently a rarity amongst country inns. Right now, there was nothing Ren wanted more than to sink into a tub of warm water and let his muscles unclench and his mind relax.

The inn corridor was dark and crammed and smelled faintly of goat. Ren found the bath at the end of the hallway, revealed by a crudely painted bucket on the door. When he pushed it open, he discovered with horror that the bath was exactly that: a bucket of water warmed over hot coals. A hole in the floor served as a drain.

Ren stared at it, contemplating for a moment whether he should just return to his and Anik's room. This sad excuse for a bath bore little resemblance to the huge, finely decorated floor tubs he knew from his home in the castle, with tiles painted blue to imitate the ocean and corners carved like golden seashells.

Still, the illusion of lingering death and the feeling of blood staining his body wouldn't leave Ren alone, so he let himself into the room and closed the door. At least a few minutes of washing his hair and body would keep him from having to think about anything else.

There was no lock on the door, and Ren half-expected someone to walk in on him with his naked body on full display. Showing off his natural state to strangers normally didn't bother him, but the thought of being called out as the bastard prince of Frayne and arrested by town guards with his bare ass covered in soap was less than appealing. Ren washed quickly, but no one entered.

"The bath is free," Ren murmured as he returned to their room, rubbing his damp hair dry with a towel. He was dressed in the same clothes he had been riding in, but felt at least a little cleaner. "The serving boy is fetching more water. It should be warm in a few minutes."

Anik had rolled up the map and moved to sit on the window sill, gaze focused on the road below. He didn't turn to look at Ren, simply acknowledged the offer with a grunt. He was still only wearing dark trousers, his chest and feet bare. Ren huffed and shook his head. He hadn't expected Anik to take him up on the offer. It wouldn't surprise Ren if Lowlanders only bathed once or twice a year.

Returning to his bed, he lay down on his side, dragging the blankets up over his shoulders. Maybe if he could stop thinking about blood, he'd finally be able to sleep.

* * *

Ren had no idea how much time had passed, but it was completely dark in the room when Anik nudged him awake.

"They're here." Anik's voice sounded close to him in the darkness.

Ren rubbed his eyes and pushed up onto his elbows. He watched the silhouette of Anik's body as Anik returned to his spot at the window. Ren looked at the other bed. It was untouched. Anik must have sat there for hours in the darkness.

Sitting up, Ren lit the candle by the side of the bed, squinting in the sudden light. As he sat up, the door opened with a soft creak. A head poked in, then the door opened the rest of the way and Niklas and Berin stepped inside. Niklas came straight for Ren and wrapped his arms tight around him.

"Are you all right?" Ren asked, squeezing Niklas to him before holding him out at arm's length to look him over, relief washing over him.

Niklas nodded, sitting down on the edge of the bed next to Ren. "Everything is chaos back home. Sneaking out wasn't too hard."

Berin came up to them, expression full of worry. He looked like he had hardly slept, the light of the candle casting dark shadows on his face.

Ren couldn't help but feel a little guilty. He was the one who had sneaked into the party; he had brought this upon himself, and consequently, his friends. "I'm sorry," he whispered, turning his eyes to the floor.

Berin gripped his shoulders tight, giving him a little shake. "Don't be sorry, boy. This wasn't your fault. The Skarlans were the ones who brought death to our city. We should never have let them through the gates." Letting go of Ren, Berin spat on the floor.

"Skarlans can never be trusted," Niklas said.

Ren smiled. In a way, they were all bastards. Berin and Niklas were both born in Skarlan, of Skarlan blood, but they had as much dislike for their neighbours to the west as any true-born Fraynean. Ren would trust both of them with his life. "What's happening at home?" Ren asked.

Berin and Niklas exchanged a look. It was Berin who spoke first. "Halvard is marrying his daughter to Thais."

It took a moment for the words to process in Ren's mind. He had almost forgotten about the Skarlan princess Evalyne. At the party, she had seemed quiet and reserved.

"Everyone was saying that Halvard would offer his daughter to Hellic," Ren said, his breath catching painfully when he spoke his brother's name. "Why this? Hel... He was the crown prince."

Berin sighed heavily and ran a hand through his hair, sitting down opposite Ren on Anik's untouched bed. "Thais doesn't come of age for another four years. I think this was Halvard's plan all along. A marriage between his daughter and Thais means that Halvard can step in as regent of Frayne until Thais can become king, all in the name of protecting the nation."

"He put on a grand performance in the courtyard this morning," Niklas said. There was poison in his tone. "Announced to everyone how he was doing it to help protect the young prince and keep the nation safe. Complete bullshit."

"Did the court believe it?" Ren asked, looking between the two of them.

"They don't have to believe it," Berin said with a sigh. "Halvard just needs to be able to point the finger at you. According to him, the fact that you ran only adds evidence to your guilt."

Ren braced his elbows against his knees and let his head hang. His mind was so full of so many different emotions, he felt it might explode. Four years. Something told him Thais would never make it to twenty.

"So what now?" Niklas asked quietly.

Ren shook his head. Callun had relatives in Aleria, but the king hadn't been born into the royal family. He had married Ren's mother around the time Ren had been born, and now that he was dead, his family would all be stripped of their titles.

"What about my uncle?" Ren asked, the thought striking him suddenly. He raised his head. "Lord Tyke, in Stag's Run. He's the queen's brother, so he has a claim to the throne. If he returned to Aleria, he could claim regency in Halvard's stead."

For the first time, Berin's eyes seemed to light up. "That could work, but you'll need to be quick about it. I heard from the guards last night that Halvard is planning to send a force to Stag's Run to secure it. If he doesn't already know the queen's brother rules there, he'll find out soon."

"What's so special about Stag's Run?" Anik asked, making himself known for the first time since Niklas and Berin had arrived. He hopped off the window sill and came towards them, crossing his arms over his chest. Niklas glared at him.

"Stag's Run is a narrow passage that leads to the North. Haven't you heard of it?" Ren asked.

"The North?" Anik said. "That huge no-man's land covered in ice and snow?"

"It's full of resources," Ren explained. "Timber, stone, minerals in the earth, wildlife. The fortress at Stag's Run guards the only entrance. It's deep in Fraynean territory, but Halvard has always been eager to gain access to it."

"And imagine what he could do with it," Berin said. "Skarlan to the west, Frayne to the east, and an unlimited supply of resources to the north."

"Now that's terrifying." Niklas shivered.

"We'll just have to get there before he does," Ren said, determination fuelling his decision. They had a goal. Everything wasn't hopeless, not yet.

Standing, Berin crossed over to the window, looking left and right down the road. "Travel with caution," he said. "King Halvard will no doubt spread word of your guilt and there'll be people out looking for you. Ride to Isleya and stock up there first."

"I'll be careful," Ren said, swallowing hard. He knew Niklas and Berin couldn't come with him. He'd be making this journey with no friends at his back. Berin had a wife and daughter in Aleria and he couldn't leave them. Niklas knew the castle well, so he'd be of more use there, watching over Thais, than trailing around after Ren. Ren knew all of this. Still, he couldn't help the dark pit of dread that spread in his stomach.

Stepping back towards them, Berin pulled the flap of his long coat aside. Two swords were strapped to Berin's hip. Ren was about to ask what they were for when Berin loosened one of the sheaths and handed it to him.

Ren recognized it immediately, and the sight of it sent a jolt of pain through him. With trembling hands, he reached out and wrapped his fingers around the leather-wrapped hilt, the curving antlers protecting his hand as he drew the sword from its sheath. It was perfectly balanced, with hardly a graze in the steel. Hellic had never gotten the chance to use it in a real battle. It was as sharp as the day it had been forged, the golden stag's head pommel glowing in the candlelight.

"Thank you," Ren said, speaking past the lump forming in his throat as he slid the sword back into its sheath and placed it against the foot of the bed.

"Keep your head up, son," Berin said, giving his shoulder a squeeze. "Things are a lot different now and I know everything looks dire, but we'll find a way to sort it out."

Ren turned to Niklas, who drew him in for a kiss on the cheek. Ren felt his hand at the back of his neck, keeping him from pulling away.

Niklas' words were a whisper. "Get rid of the slave, Ren."

"Take care of yourself," Ren answered.

Silence fell once more as the door closed behind Berin and Niklas. Ren watched them from the window, feeling utterly alone. When he turned away, he glanced at Anik, who had lain down on his own bed, feet crossed. His eyes were closed.

* * *

With the first rays of early morning sunlight, Ren and Anik left the inn behind. Letting his horse drink from the trough, Ren tightened the girth and then swung himself into the saddle. He shot a sidelong glance at Anik. Anik stroked his horse's nose and held up a hand, letting it munch on the slices of carrot in his palm. Ren hadn't seen him taking the carrot from their breakfast meal. At least he hadn't made Ren pay for the extra treats for his horse.

Ren knew the slave would try to leave, and he knew he would have to stop him. Anik might be a Lowland warrior, but Ren would simply have to be firm.

"Well, good luck, I guess," Anik said, as he swung into the saddle and turned his horse towards the open fields.

"I can't let you leave," Ren said, turning after him and guiding his horse alongside Anik's.

Anik didn't slow. "Like I said, to the town and no further. This is the town. My debt is paid."

"I don't know how to navigate. I don't even know where to go from here. I haven't freed you of your service," Ren argued, nudging his horse forward to cut Anik off.

Anik easily dodged and replied by tossing Ren the rolled up map from the inn.

Ren caught it and stared at it. "I've never read a map before. I'm ordering you to stay."

"Oh, for fuck's sake," Anik groaned, stopping his horse and wheeling it around so he could face Ren. "Look, Prince I'm-So-Important. You're no longer my problem and I don't care what happens to you, so piss off and leave me alone." He heeled his horse into a gallop and Ren watched him leave with a growing sense of panic. This wasn't how it was supposed to go.

"You're still my slave. Stop at once!" Ren shouted, but Anik didn't slow. He didn't even seem to have heard.

Groaning with frustration, Ren kicked his horse into a gallop and chased Anik down. It was time to change his tactics.

Reaching out, he gripped the reins of Anik's horse, making it twist its neck to the side and come to an awkward halt.

"Let go of my horse," Anik snapped.

Ren squared his shoulders. "Don't you want revenge for what Halvard has done to you? For making you a slave?"

Anik went quiet, his jaw tensing. Finally, something seemed to have gotten through to him. That intense fury Ren had seen in his eyes back in the dungeons had returned, although it didn't seem to be directed at him this time.

Around them, those of Teu's citizens awake and working in the fields in the early morning shot them concerned glances. A woman grabbed a young girl by the arm and tugged her farther from the road.

Anik drew a deep breath and Ren dared to let go of his reins.

"Fine. I'll babysit you as far as Stag's Run, castle boy. But these are the conditions." Anik's voice dripped with contempt. He pressed his horse all the way up against Ren's.

Ren nearly fell from the saddle when Anik gripped the front of his jacket and yanked him in close.

"I'm not your slave and you don't get to order me around. I'll

67

follow you to the gates of the fortress and then you'll never see me again."

"Fine," Ren said, yanking his jacket from Anik's grip.

Anik turned his horse around once more, the agitated command making it huff nervously. "Fine."

Ren didn't care if Anik was furious with him. He had gotten what he wanted.

CHAPTER FOUR

They rode out of Teu as the sun made its slow journey across the sky. Ren had to purchase a shirt and jacket for Anik to wear, along with a pair of boots. It wasn't too cold for him to ride shirtless, but the Lowlander tattoo on his arm drew more attention than Ren liked. If Skarlan guards came riding this way asking for them, at least two dozen villagers would be able to tell them where Ren and Anik had gone, even if they might not help a Skarlan soldier until a sword was held to their throats. Ren didn't want these people to risk their lives because he had been careless.

It was strange travelling like this. In Aleria, everyone knew Ren by sight and greeted him with smiles and friendly gestures. Here, with the hood casting his face into shadow and with only a single foreign man as a companion, hardly anyone spared him a glance. Once, Ren almost rode down several people, expecting the group of travellers to scatter around him. Except they didn't, which earned Ren quite a few colourful curses spat at his back as he hurried past. He was more careful, after that.

When the sun reached its highest point in the sky, Anik steered his horse away form the road and in between the golden wheat in direction of the hedgerows. "We need to get off the road," he said. "The first places guards search are along the roads."

Ren was almost relieved to leave the busy road behind in favour of the narrow riding trails that lined fields and creeks. He followed Anik, who seemed to have no problem figuring out which direction to go. Anik didn't speak to him, except to give him directions in a clipped tone of voice. He sighed at Ren when he lagged behind and snapped whenever Ren questioned his chosen path. Ren tried to tell himself he shouldn't expect any kind of compassion or even civility from a Lowlander, but it made him long more than anything for the pleasant company of the soft and friendly castle slaves. At least now, he knew why Frayneans never bought Lowlander slaves. It was beyond him why Skarlan would ever choose to cultivate them. Then again, little of what Skarlans did ever made sense to Ren. Maybe they enjoyed getting regularly insulted. That thought, at least, brought a smile of amusement to Ren's face.

It was twilight once more before they stopped to rest. Anik slowed down his mare and pointed to a sheltered spot by the river, a patch of grass hidden from sight by large bushes. Ren brought his horse to a stop and swung out of the saddle. When his feet hit the ground, his legs buckled, sharp bolts of pain shooting through his muscles and he groaned, clinging to the saddle with both hands.

"Not used to riding, are you?" Anik commented as he passed by Ren, a smug smile on his face. Ren ignored him.

Carefully, Ren straightened his aching legs. His muscles were sore and the skin on the insides of his thighs felt rubbed raw from the saddle. He found himself grateful that Stag's Run was less than a week's ride away.

Without saying a word to Ren, Anik wandered off to gather firewood and Ren made himself busy unloading his bags from his horse and refilling the water skins. It wasn't easy to ignore the ache in his muscles, and it made his walk awkwardly stiff.

Ren was surprised how much work was involved in setting up camp. Preparing a place to sleep, building a fire, making food…they were all things he was used to letting other people handle. It took Ren twice as long as it should have to clear a spot for a fire, and after that, Anik stopped asking him to do stuff, which suited Ren just fine. He was happy to simply sit and rest his legs while Anik handled the rest.

The last of the daylight was nearly gone when Anik stepped down to the water's edge, discarding his boots and rolling up his trousers. Ren watched him silently, sitting close to the warmth of the fire as Anik waded carefully into the water and positioned himself in the middle of the river, legs slightly bent and hands stretched out in front of himself. Ren frowned. About a minute passed. Then a sudden splash made Ren jump and he watched with wide eyes as Anik pulled a wiggling fish out of the water with both hands.

"Whoa, that was amazing," Ren exclaimed, staring in awe as Anik waded out of the water and brought the fish back to the fire. He placed it on a rock, holding it still with one hand.

Anik kept his eyes on the fish and extended a hand towards Ren. "Your knife."

Quickly, Ren drew it from his belt and handed it over. As he watched, Anik stabbed the knife into the fish with practised ease, severing its head. His lips moved with whispered words too quiet for Ren to hear. Then, he went about gutting and cleaning his catch, legs crossed and sleeves rolled up to expose the dark ink on his skin.

Ren watched him as he worked. Anik's hands were stained with the fish's blood and a few stray strands of hair had fallen loose from the leather tie and hung over his face. Like this, Anik certainly lived up to all the descriptions of Lowlanders Ren had ever heard.

"Here," Anik said, grabbing the fish by the tail and slapping it down on the grass between Ren's feet.

Ren stared at it. "What am I supposed to do with it?" he asked, picking it up by the tail the same way Anik had done it.

"Well," Anik said slowly, eyes narrowing at Ren as if he wasn't entirely sure if Ren was being serious. "My first suggestion would be to de-bone it."

"De-..."

"Don't tell me you've never de-boned a fish?" Anik asked. His eyebrows shot up. When Ren said nothing, Anik let out an exasperated sigh. "Seriously?" He reached across the flames of the fire to snatch the fish from Ren's hand. Using Ren's knife, he sliced along the back of the fish, picked it apart and tugged on the spine with more force than Ren suspected was entirely necessary. Anik pulled the entire length of it free from the fish's flesh before turning his attention to the smaller bones.

"So," Ren started, in attempt to kill the new, awkward, stony silence. "What was your life like before all this?"

Anik looked up from the fish, glaring at Ren with a pair of honey-brown eyes that Ren thought were far too pretty to belong in such a grumpy face, then turned his attention back to his work. "I don't want to talk."

Ren raised an eyebrow. "You don't want to talk right now, or you don't want to talk at all?"

"I don't want to talk to *you*," Anik corrected.

Ren shook his head and sighed. Around them, it was getting darker, the fire casting long, dancing shadows along the ground. "So, what, we're going to hate each other all the way to Stag's Run?"

"Fine by me," Anik said, slicing the fish into two even pieces before setting them down on the rocks close to the fire.

Ren stared at him, feeling his annoyance building again. "So it's completely impossible for you to be just a little nice to people who are nice to you?"

Anik copied his glare. "Listen here, skahli. I'm not your friend and I don't want to be friends with someone like you, so let's quit the small talk."

"Someone like me?" Ren asked, lip curling.

"Yes, someone like you," Anik repeated, wiping Ren's knife clean of fish blood with a ferocity that was disconcerting, only to sink the blade hilt-deep into the soil. "High-and-mighty assholes who think it's their right to order other people around just because they were lucky enough to be born with gold pouring out of their ears. I know exactly what your kind is like. You don't give a shit about the rest of us, and even if I explained it to you, you would never understand." Anik rearranged the stones in the fire with his bare hands, yanking his hand back when the flames licked at his fingers. Then he slapped the two even slices of the fish down onto the stones to cook.

74

Ren felt a sharp reply burning on his tongue, but he swallowed it again. Anik was currently handling his dinner, after all. To be honest, he was handling a lot more than that. Without him, Ren would be lost. He only had to endure Anik's unfriendly attitude for a handful of days. "Lowlanders," he murmured to himself.

They ate in a tense, uncomfortable silence. The fish provided a tasteless meal under a dark sky on the damp, cold ground, Ren picking strips of meat off his slice of fish with his fingers because they had brought no eating utensils. It was as far removed from the pleasant family dinners in Aleria as one could get. Ren closed his eyes and could so clearly imagine it: the light from the fireplace; roasted pork, vegetables, gravy, and potatoes on the table; Hellic telling them all about how impressed the castle sword-master was with his footwork. Fuck, Ren even missed Thais' obnoxious attempts at trying to kick his legs under the table. He opened his eyes when he felt his throat tighten.

Anik was up from his seat already, seemingly uninterested in keeping Ren's company any longer than necessary. Ren watched him out of the corner of his eye as he got up from his seat, cleaned his hands in the river and returned to his chosen sleeping spot, crawling into the makeshift cocoon of blankets he had made for himself. Anik didn't lie down to sleep right away. Rather, he slipped off his boots once more and dropped his jacket on the ground, then moved a few feet away from the fire. As Ren watched, he began to move in the dim glow of the dancing light.

It was hypnotizing, his movements slow, yet precise, like something between a dance and a fight against an invisible opponent. The muscles of his back rippled and cast shadows over his skin as he moved slowly, then quickly, then slowly again. Ren had no idea what he was doing. It didn't look like any combat training he had ever seen. Ren felt his eyelids grow heavy, Anik's movements and the faint sounds of his measured breaths and soft footsteps on the grass lulling Ren to sleep. He slept through the night for the first time in days.

* * *

Anik woke Ren with the first rays of daylight and they were back on the road before the sun had even risen above the trees. Ren hadn't expected the muscles of his calves and thighs to feel even more sore than the day before, and he grimaced as he swung himself into the saddle. He remained quiet, however. The last thing he wanted to do was confirm Anik's accusations of weakness. Still, the chafing of the leather saddle against his sensitive thighs made him wince as Anik set the pace to a brisk walk.

They rode over rolling hills and across green and yellow fields. Ren had travelled this stretch of land a few times before when his family had business in Isleya or during rare summer vacations, but seeing the countryside from horseback was entirely different from riding in a carriage along the road. Either that, or his lack of a conversation partner simply made him pay more attention to his surroundings. All around them, the land was rich with life. They even had to stop their horses to let a herd of deer spring across their path. There were at least thirty of the animals, including two stags with beautiful, curving antlers. Ren lingered, watching them race for the trees as Anik rode on ahead.

After a few hours of riding, the subtle slope of the terrain became more apparent. They were ascending steadily higher above sea level. Berin had told him once that Stag's Run was covered in snow almost all year where it lay nestled between the mountains, but here, late summer still dominated. It would be a few days before they would really start to feel the cold.

The sun was setting once more by the time they rode into Isleya. The city spread out before them like an ant's nest: a large cluster of buildings and houses surrounded by open fields with a market in its centre drawing the attention of the crowd. Isleya was more than three times the size of Teu, with wide streets, decorated fountains, and a large arena for sports and entertainment. Ren had visited the city with his family on more than one occasion. The decennial grand horse race hosted in Isleya drew crowds from all over Frayne and the south-eastern nations. Ren had been sixteen the last time it was held, a youth full of energy and wonder. The race had seemed like the world's greatest event and the attention he had received had left him floating for days.

Now, as they rode their horses through the busy streets, the hood of Ren's jacket covering half his face, no one spared them a glance. No giggling young men and women threw flowers and called out his name, no merchants and travellers nodded their heads at him in respect. Instead, Ren was left to weave his way through a crowd of people who were much too busy with their daily tasks and chores to pay him any attention. It had been like this in Teu, but the effect seemed somehow amplified in a city as large and busy as Isleya. Even here, gold and white ribbons billowed from flag poles all along the widest roads in honour of the crown prince's birthday. To Ren, the bright strips of fabric were nothing but a grim and mocking reminder.

Ren knew it was risky to come here, but they desperately needed supplies for their journey. Besides, it had been several years since Ren had last visited. If he kept his head down, he'd be okay. Probably. No one would expect a prince to ride alone and unannounced.

The inn was close to the market. Twice the size of the one in Teu and newly renovated, it was crowded with people singing and dancing and farmers enjoying their dinner. As Ren accepted the key to their room, a group of men and women playing cards burst into cheers and laughter. It struck Ren that none of them had any idea of the horrors that had turned the fate of their country upside down just a few days earlier. It felt almost like an insult that these people could smile and dance when their beloved crown prince was lying still and cold in the soil. Ren hadn't even been able to attend his funeral.

"It's all a bit too much if you ask me." One man's rough voice carried over the other patrons'. "How much fucking gold and silk does one spoiled brat need? I wonder how long it takes before they run out of gift ideas. What do you even give a prince who already owns a thousand horses and three-hundred holes to fuck?"

"Oh, shut up, Villum," a woman said, smacking down her row of cards on the table, making Villum let out an exasperated groan and swipe his own set off the table and onto the floor. "The kid only turns twenty once," she continued. "If he wants another two dozen bed boys, I say let him. So long as it isn't my sons."

"I don't know," a second lady said, grinning at the others. "He could fuck my sons if he wanted to, so long as he married them afterwards."

Ren stared at them, something like anger bubbling inside him. He started forward, but a hand on his arm stopped him in his tracks. Anik's grip on him was tight and when Ren met his eyes, Anik shook his head.

Ren slowly released the tension in his body. It wouldn't be long before the news reached Isleya. Maybe another day or two. Uncertainty and fear would fill these people's lives before long. They deserved to enjoy this carefree happiness while they still could.

Ren ordered dinner and a room at the bar, eyes downcast and voice hushed. Anywhere else, the unusual behaviour of a cloaked stranger might have raised suspicion, but in a town as busy as Isleya, the innkeeper didn't bat an eye. With the door to their rented room locked safely behind them, Ren discarded his jacket and loosened the ties of his undershirt. After the dry and tasteless fish from the night before, the steaming lamb stew served by the inn's cook made his taste buds sing. Judging by the look in Anik's eyes when Ren had ordered the most expensive thing on the menu, he clearly thought it was a waste of money, but Ren couldn't care less. Anik ate Ren's meal of choice without complaint. It was a luxury worth paying for. They likely wouldn't get to eat food cooked in a proper kitchen again until they reached Stag's Run. Staying in towns was becoming too much of a risk.

"You should get rid of those," Anik said, resting his bowl against his thigh before pointing to Ren's ear. They were the first words Anik had spoken to him since ordering him out of bed that morning, and for a moment, Ren simply gawked at him. Then, slowly, he raised his hand to his own ear, fingering the golden stud earrings. His title was in those little pieces of gold. Bastard prince of Frayne. With a soft sigh, he took them out one by one and slipped them into his pocket. Anik had a point; everyone in Frayne knew what those earrings meant.

Ren's gaze lingered on Anik, an unanswered question burning on his tongue. "Back in Aleria," he started. "What happened? Where did you get the knife?"

Anik tilted his head, as if trying to decide whether to indulge him or not. Taking a mouthful of stew, he swallowed before answering. "King Halvard's advisor planted it on me before they brought me out."

"Nathair?"

"Yes."

Ren looked him up and down. He thought about how long it would take to assassinate two men and then hide the weapon on a slave in the other end of the castle. Hellic and Callun had been dead before Ren had even entered the garden. When Ren had bumped into Halvard and Nathair in the dungeons, Nathair had already been carrying the knife one of the Hakvard's men had used to kill his family. The thought chilled him to the bone and he fell silent.

After finishing their food, Ren took their empty bowls and placed them on a tray outside the door. Anik lit an oil lamp and brought it with him. Then, they sat down on the floor with the map stretched out between them.

"We need to stay off the road," Anik said, voice hushed in the silence. His long hair was ruffled, loose strands framing the sides of his face. Ren wondered if he ever loosened it to brush it.

"Of course," Ren said, eyes following the path Anik drew with a finger from their current location to Stag's Run in the north.

"It looks about five or six days' ride away. Let's make it five. We need supplies. Food, water-"

"Coats," Ren interrupted. "And gloves."

Anik glanced up at him.

"You said it yourself," Ren continued. "The north is covered in ice and snow. If you think it's chilly now, just wait until we reach the mountains. The cold can kill."

"Very well," Anik said, turning his attention back to the map. "We'll pick up supplies tomorrow morning and leave as soon as we're done."

Ren stared at him for a moment. He had almost expected an argument, maybe because it felt like every single conversation they'd had since their escape had turned into one. But this was nice. They were talking, agreeing. Ren could almost pretend that Anik didn't hate his guts. Almost.

* * *

The streets of Isleya were busy even in the early hours of the morning. Ren had hoped to avoid the worst of it by going out just before the break of dawn, but the people here were apparently ridiculously early risers. It was nerve-wracking, men and women casting brief glances in Ren's direction as they passed. He wore his jacket with the hood pulled up, but he still felt like every person might stop and shout his name in recognition.

Anik, who walked next to him, drew just as much attention. The crowd withdrew from him like mice spotting a hawk every time he opened his mouth to speak. Without the tattoo on his arm visible, he could blend in, but his accent was unmistakable. As in Aleria, people in Isleya were used to seeing Lowlanders as children and beggars in side alleys, not as tall, strong, young men walking in their midst. Besides, the most common expression on Anik's face was cold displeasure. No wonder people moved out of his way. A few slightly braver men and women hissed curses as he passed or spat on the ground at his feet before darting away quickly.

"I'm not the only one at risk of drawing the wrong kind of attention," Ren noted sourly.

"I've noticed," Anik replied, seemingly unfazed, and continued ahead.

Colourful stalls in all shapes and sizes lined the plaza around them, engulfing them in a vivid mix of scents, sights, and sounds. They made their way methodically through their list of required items, passing women loudly proclaiming their selections of fruits and vegetables and a man trying to get people to buy chickens by stuffing them into the arms of unsuspecting passersbys. Ren dodged a chicken thrust at his chest by slipping underneath the head of a mule pulling a cart through the crowd.

They bought food, coats, extra blankets, and an additional

water skin. With a coat draped over his arm, Ren drew a gold coin from his pocket and paid an elderly merchant for two pairs of fur-lined boots. Every time he approached a merchant, the fear of recognition made his heart skip a beat, but he couldn't exactly let Anik do the talking.

Ren stuffed the boots into his brimming travel bag. He had given Anik Keelan's bag, rearranging the contents of both to fit their new purchases. As Ren went over their list of items in his head one last time, an old woman stepped into his path, dangling a necklace with a heavy crystal pendant in front of his face. He almost bumped right into her, and for a moment, the fear of recognition sent a cold shiver down Ren's back. But the woman's eyes were entirely glazed over, her gaze unfocused. Despite it, she reached out and locked her hands around both his and Anik's wrists with surprising precision.

"Your wedding is going to be glorious," she proclaimed, nodding knowingly.

Ren glanced between her and Anik, taken completely aback by her unexpected declaration.

"Care to purchase a pendant for good luck?" she continued, stuffing the heavy necklace into Ren's palm.

Ren wiggled his hand out of her grip and took a step back. "Sorry, you're mistaken. We're not getting married," he said. "I don't want to buy anything."

"Oh, you silly boy," she said, reaching up with both hands in an attempt to drape the necklace around his neck instead. "This pendant will help you with your denial."

Ren ducked just in time, slipping past the old woman before she could try to force any more of her good luck charms on him. Blowing out a breath, he rolled his eyes and returned his thoughts to the day's task, stopping beside a sugar apple stall to collect his thoughts, the sweet scent of the sugar making his stomach growl. He added breakfast to his mental list. Next to him, Anik smirked and leaned against the stall's wooden support pillar, clearly amused.

"All right, I think we should-" A tug on his cloak made Ren freeze and he spun around only to stumble over the feet of a young girl who quickly drew her hand out of his pocket. She looked up at him with eyes as round as teacups, wringing her hands in front of her chest.

"S-spare a coin, sir?" she asked in a thick Lowlander accent. Her voice trembled and her face was streaked with dirt, her pale hair tangled. Behind her, a boy even smaller than her was hiding and clinging to her arm, his feet bare against the cobblestones.

Ren looked up to see Anik watching him closely, but before he could make a move, a broom came swinging into his field of vision and Ren staggered back a step.

"Get out of here, you thieving rats," the candy apple stall merchant hissed, waving his broom at the children, who scattered and disappeared into an alley.

Ren tore his gaze away from the scene, eager to escape the countless sets of eyes suddenly trained on him. The merchant said something, but Ren didn't hear what it was as he squeezed between two stalls and out onto the other side. He didn't miss the way a pair of guards in white uniforms turned their heads towards the sound of the disturbance. He tugged the hood of his jacket further down over his face.

"What are children even doing running around alone on the streets?" Ren murmured, looking over his shoulder as they made their way past a wood carver and a trinket seller trying to drown each other out with declarations of cheap prices. Ren placed the coin purse in his inner pocket, out of the way of small, grabby hands.

"Let me know if you want me to actually enlighten you on the harsh realities of life on the streets," Anik said, a step behind Ren.

Ren's brow furrowed. "Forget I asked." He stopped by a a baker's stall, paying for two ham-and-tomato buns, still warm from the oven. He handed one of them to Anik, brushing aside the unpleasant thoughts of starving children. "All right, I think we're done. We can get the horses and get out of here."

"No, wait," Anik said. He wrapped both hands around his bun to warm them before taking a bite.

"What?" Ren asked, impatience making the word come out clipped. The longer they stayed, the greater the chance of them getting their throats slit.

"I need a weapon."

"Absolutely not," Ren protested. "Slaves don't carry weapons."

Anik fixed him with one of those looks that seemed able to turn rock into molten lava. "Didn't I tell you, already? Enough with the slave crap."

Ren felt a twinge of nervousness and hated himself for it.

"Yeah, because it won't be suspicious at all to see an armed Lowlander strolling down the street," he countered sharply.

Anik raised his eyebrows at Ren. "Well then, I can just leave you to deal with all the soldiers and guards that'll come chasing us down while I take a nice, relaxing nap by the river. It's not as though your life matters to me." He turned and started back in direction of their horses.

Ren swallowed, feeling heat rise in his cheeks. He had always considered the art of talking one of his finest skills, but Anik seemed to keep yanking that rug out from underneath him. He sighed. "Fine, I'll buy you a weapon."

They left the busy marketplace behind in search of a smithy. Ren was thankful for the thinning of the crowd around him, even if Isleya's streets were still busier than those in Teu. The architecture in the city's wealthy districts, made mostly of light sandstone buildings and engraved arches, reminded Ren of Aleria. Here, thankfully, there were no golden ribbons on flagpoles or above doorways to remind Ren of his misery.

They found the smithy by following the sound of struck iron. When they arrived, the smith greeted them from beneath the belly of a large bay draft horse.

"I'm looking for a sword," Ren explained.

The smith lowered the horse's massive front hoof to the ground before turning towards them. "Over there's what I have for sale," he said, pointing to a rack with his hammer. "If you want something custom-made, it'll take about a week."

"Thank you," Ren said, sitting down on a rough stone bench as Anik wandered over to inspect the selection.

Ren ate his bun while he waited. It took Anik an unreasonable amount of time to select a weapon. Determining balance and weight was apparently a timely process and extremely important to the Lowlander. It reminded Ren of when Danali'd had to pick new curtains for Thais' room last year after Thais had accidentally set the old ones on fire. Ren had never known there could be so many different kinds of fabrics, stitchings, and patterns. And just like the curtains, he could hardly tell the difference between the various swords Anik tried to choose from as he held them out in front of him, smoothed a hand down the lengths of the blades and swung them at invisible enemies.

"This one," Anik said finally, swinging the fifth sword of the bunch in a slow circle. Tossing the sword into the air, he allowed it to make a full turn before catching it by the hilt.

Ren rolled his eyes. "Fine. How much?" he asked the smith, pushing off the bench and fishing his pouch of money out of his pocket.

"Ten gold," the smith said, and Ren passed over the coins and pulled his bag over his shoulder once more, ready to get out of there before they pushed their luck too far.

"Ten gold is too much," Anik said as they left the smithy together. "You should have haggled."

"Oh, now you're concerned about my economic situation? You made me pay fifteen for a map," Ren reminded him.

"Well I'm not the one who scoffs at freshly caught fish, so I don't care if you can't afford any more of your fancy dinners."

Ren clenched his jaw, eyes narrowed. He stopped and turned. "Seriously? Are you really going to complain about me all the way to Stag's Run? I just bought you a sword you don't even deserve, so can you please stop criticizing me for five minutes?"

Anik's entire body tensed. Chest to chest like this, the height difference between them seemed even greater than it was. But before either of them could say another word, a new voice made Ren's heart skip a beat.

"Prince Ren! Is that you? The young Stag! I haven't seen you since my father's autumn feast three years ago."

The voice belonged to a young man with neatly combed dark brown hair and a jacket heavily embroidered with gold thread. Ren knew him well; had bedded him more than once. He was pleasant and kind, but right now, he was the last person Ren wanted to see.

Ren tried to turn away, but the young man caught Ren by the shoulder and opened his arms for a friendly embrace. "What a coincidence. What are you doing out here by yourself? Sneaking out again? If you could be tempted, I know just the place-"

"Lord Scyan, I..." Ren held up both hands to try and stop him from coming closer, but the damage was already done. From the corner of his eye, Ren saw heads turn and hands move to sword hilts. The golden cuffs of guards' jackets caught the sunlight as they turned towards them, glanced between each other and then reached for their swords.

Anik's hand closed tight around Ren's wrist as the sharp voices of the guards echoed between the buildings. Anik wasn't looking at him, but at the three mounted guards suddenly blocking the way they had come. Messenger birds had flown faster than their horses had walked. "We need to run. Now," he said.

"We can't outrun horses," Ren hissed, backing up. He could feel his heart beating in his throat.

Lord Scyan looked between them and the guards, confusion and uncertainty shining in his eyes.

"Now, Ren!" Anik shouted, before turning on his heel and sprinting back towards the market. An arrow bounced off the cobblestones where his feet had been only a second ago. Ren didn't linger.

CHAPTER FIVE

Bolting down the street as fast as he could, Ren pushed past stalls and people, carts and horses. Behind him, the guards were forced to wheel their mounts around to keep from barrelling into the crowd. Anik was ahead of him, and led the way in between buildings and over a fence. Chickens scattered and flapped their wings in fear as they fled through the streets. Ren could hear shouts and several sets of hooves clattering against stone. No matter what they did to try and shake them, the guards knew the streets well. In a matter of minutes, every guard in the town would be chasing them.

Ren's heart hammered in his chest, breath burning in his lungs. He skipped around an elderly man in his path carrying a crate of fruit and turned a corner. Anik was gone. Ren stopped, frantically spinning around. Which way now? The shouts were getting closer. It couldn't end like this. If he could just find a place to hide...

A tight grip on his arm yanked him backward and he let out a surprised yelp as he was dragged through an opening in a fence.

Anik pulled Ren down behind a pair of large barrels only moments before the horses came thundering by. He could feel Anik's hot breath against his neck before the Lowlander let go of him, his gaze lingering for a moment before he pushed to his feet.

They both froze.

They were in a backyard, a few chickens scraping at the muddy ground around their feet. Everything was grey and brown, dry dirt covering the ground and the lower part of the wall, making the young man clutching a bag of corn to his chest look completely out of place. He appeared to be about eighteen and had a beautiful face, long blond hair falling over his shoulder in a soft wave. His large, frightened eyes were cornflower blue. The iron cuffs around his wrists looked too big and too rough for his delicate frame.

"Don't scream," Anik said quietly, holding up both hands like he was trying to calm a frightened animal. The boy's breathing was shallow, lips parting as his eyes darted to the swords at their hips, but he kept quiet.

"What's taking so long, boy?" a deep, rough voice called from inside, making the youth flinch. Ren heard footsteps, then the

92

creaking of hinges as the door to the backyard opened. A large, broad-shouldered man wearing a bloody apron appeared in the doorway. Ren's eyes widened at the massive cleaver in his hand.

Anik was the first to move, reaching for his sword, but Ren closed a hand around his wrist and squeezed before he got a chance to draw.

"We need a place to lie low for a bit," Ren said, shining a disarming smile at the butcher. "We won't be any trouble, and we will pay you for the inconvenience, of course," he continued, reaching for his rapidly thinning money pouch with his free hand and drawing a few golden coins out to display to the stranger.

With the lure of gold, it only took the butcher a moment to decide, and a warm, welcoming smile spread on his face. "Please, come inside."

* * *

"The name's Rowland," the butcher said, leading Ren and Anik into the back of his shop, which seemed to serve both as a workplace and a living area. Ren made a wide berth around three pig halves hanging from hooks in the ceiling. To the left was the shopfront, where yet more meat was lined up along the counter, although most of the day's stock seemed to have sold out already. Through a door to the right was a small sitting area and a kitchen, as well as a narrow flight of stairs Ren assumed led up to

Rowland's sleeping quarters.

"I'm, uh, Niklas. This is Anik," Ren said, pointing over his shoulder. "Thanks for letting us stay," he continued, handing over the gold coins. "We-"

"I don't need to know," Rowland interrupted, giving Ren a stern look as he pocketed the gold. "Silence all around is better for everyone. Make yourselves comfortable." He gestured towards the open door that led to the sitting area, then turned his attention to the blond boy. "Come on, don't just stand there. Get our guests something to drink."

The place was worn down, but kept clean. There was not a speck of dust on the surface of the small table between them. A faint smell of blood hung on the air, wafting in from the shop front.

"Looks like we got lucky," Ren said, and dropped his bag on the floor before taking a seat in the nearest chair. "Thanks for taking off without me, you ass."

Anik ignored him. He wasn't even looking at him. Instead, he was watching the boy place cups of water onto a tray in the small kitchen, gaze intense.

"What?" Ren asked.

"You don't think it's odd?" Anik asked in a low voice. His whole body was tense and his eyes didn't leave the boy. "What's a butcher doing with a slave like that?"

Ren followed his gaze. He hadn't thought about it until now, but Anik was right. The boy was beautiful, elegant and long-limbed, hair gleaming in the last of the daylight that shone through the windows. He looked like he belonged in a palace, not a butcher shop. As he came towards them with the tray, Ren noticed something else – above the place where the heavy shackles had rubbed the boy's fine skin red, long, thin, slightly uneven scars travelled halfway up his forearms. Ren glanced at Anik, and judging by the intense fury in his eyes, he had seen it, too.

Putting down the tray, the boy quickly wrapped his arms around himself and made to leave, but Anik reached out and closed a hand around one of his slender wrists. The boy gasped, freezing in Anik's grip. Ren didn't miss the tremor that went through the youth's body, and Anik must have felt it too, for he released his grip.

"What's your name?" Anik asked.

"Ilias, my lord," the boy said softly, eyes downcast.

"I'm not a lord," Anik replied, mouth twisting.

"I-I'm sorry." Ilias' voice was barely a whisper.

Ren looked between the two of them. There was a new look in Anik's eyes. Ren had heard it, too; the slave spoke with a distinct Lowlander accent.

It was the last thing Ren had expected, and it didn't match at all with everything Ren knew about the Lowlanders. They were aggressive, brutish killers with no sense of conscience. This boy was soft and demure.

"What happened to your arms, Ilias?" Anik asked, voice softer than Ren had heard it before.

"He has a weak mind." Rowland's voice startled all three of them. He leaned against the doorway behind Ilias and stroked the boy's hair before nudging him out of the room with an elbow. "He needs someone to take care of him. Make sure he doesn't hurt himself."

"Is that why you keep him in shackles?" Anik's voice was dripping with venom. Ren almost expected him to draw his sword again when an amused smile tugged on Rowland's lips, but Anik stayed where he was.

The door to the shop opened, a chiming bell announcing the arrival of customers, and Rowland left them alone.

"I'm not staying here," Anik said, draining his cup of water before putting it down too hard on the table. Standing, he strode over to the window.

"Well, you'll have to," Ren sighed. What Ilias lacked in Lowlander stereotypes, Anik was certainly embodying.

"If I have to spend one more moment listening to that piece of-"

"The streets are crawling with guards. They'll be on the lookout for us all day," Ren reminded him. "There's no way we can fetch the horses and ride out of here without risking an arrow in the back. We have to wait until it gets dark."

Anik's grip on the window sill was white-knuckled, but he didn't argue. Ren sipped his water, listening to the murmur of voices coming from the front of the building. A few moments later, he heard the door open and close, and then footsteps approaching.

Rowland poked his head in through the doorway. "If you boys help me clean up in the shop, dinner is on me."

Ren offered the butcher a pleasant smile.

* * *

If someone had told Ren two weeks ago that he would spend an otherwise lovely late summer evening mopping blood off the floors of a back-alley butcher shop while hiding from people who wanted to kill him, he'd have thought they'd had a few too many cups of wine.

Ren had never held a mop before in his life, and had no idea using one could possibly require so much finesse. Luckily, Ilias turned out to have endless amounts of patience as he taught Ren for the third time how to actually clean the floor instead of simply pushing the blood around. Together, they worked quickly, for which Ren was thankful. The sight of the blood made his stomach turn, and he wondered briefly which slave in Aleria had been tasked with removing the evidence of his family's murder from the marble floors.

"Got to really get into the corners," Ilias said. He sat on his knees on the tiled floor and scrubbed at the panels with a wet cloth. "Otherwise the blood will start to stink something awful."

Ren looked over his shoulder at the stretch of floor he had just finished washing. Remnants of blood clung to the cracks in the tiles. He grabbed the other cloth from the bucket and got down onto his knees. He had no idea how Ilias could kneel on the hard cold floor so effortlessly. It had taken less than a minute for Ren's knees to start aching. "Doesn't it ever feel useless working so hard to clean when it's only going to get dirty again tomorrow?" he asked over his shoulder.

Ilias made a soft sound, wringing out his cloth over the bucket. "It's my job. I don't mind."

When Ren pushed back on his feet and returned to the bucket alongside him, Ilias lowered his head, cheeks flushed bright red. "I've never done housework with a free man before. You'll have to excuse me if I step out of line, my lord." Ilias' voice was soft, and coupled with his flowing Lowlander accent, Ren had to strain to understand his words.

Ren had instantly taken a liking to Ilias. Ilias reminded him of the castle slaves, and of Keelan in particular. The red-headed youth was not quite as delicate as Ilias, but they moved in the same graceful fashion that spoke of a year's careful training. There was no doubt that Ilias had been trained for finer company than Rowland.

Ren offered the youth a smile, wiping his hand clean in a dry cloth before giving the boy's shoulder a squeeze. "Not at all. You've been most pleasant."

The compliment made Ilias beam. Ren didn't miss the way Ilias seemed to gravitate towards his effortless manner of interaction. Ren knew he had to be cautious. The kind of small-village traveller he was pretending to be wouldn't know how to appreciate a slave of Ilias' quality, and Ren had no doubt that Ilias might mention this to Rowland. Ren didn't expect the butcher to keep quiet if he found out he was in fact harbouring the condemned bastard prince of Frayne and his accomplice. He wondered how much money they were offering for his head.

While Ren worked with Ilias in the back room, Anik was helping Rowland in the front, packing away leftover meat and cleaning counters. Ren kept glancing nervously in their direction, but Rowland's head remained firmly attached to his shoulders. After a while, Ren stopped worrying that there'd be trouble.

He should have known the peace wouldn't last.

Rowland had Ilias fetch extra chairs so they could all eat together in the sitting room, then took the boy into the kitchen.

Anik's fingers drummed against the small, worn table where he sat opposite Ren. Ren didn't say anything. He had spent enough time in Anik's company by now to recognize when Anik was in a bad mood.

Ren picked up his fork and absently spun it between his

fingers while they waited. Frowning slightly, he lifted the fork closer to his face, then scraped at its stained surface with a fingernail. He glanced at the plate, wondering if the concept of washing dishes with soap hadn't yet reached the smaller alleyways of Isleya. Pulling his sleeve over his hand, he rubbed at a smudge on the edge of the plate.

The sound of shattering clay made Ren jump. The sharp slap that followed had Anik out of his chair before Ren had even registered what was happening.

"Anik!" Ren rushed after him and stopped behind Anik in the doorway to the tiny kitchen.

Rowland's large frame took up most of the space in the room where he stood, face red with anger and one hand clasped tightly around the young slave's neck. On the floor between their feet lay the pieces of the shattered bowl, beef soup splattered across the wooden planks.

"It's burnt, you little piece of shit. Completely inedible. How dare you embarrass me like this in front of our guests?" Rowland's hand tightened around Ilias' throat and the boy made a desperate, choked sound. "I worked for this food and you ruined it! Do I really still have to tell you how to do everything?" Rowland released him and Ilias gasped, touching his face where a red mark was already blossoming.

Next to him, Ren felt Anik's entire body tensing. He wrapped a firm hand around Anik's wrist to keep him still. If Anik killed a man, they would never escape the city alive.

Before Ren had a chance to try to diffuse the situation, Rowland grabbed Ilias by the hair and shoved him to his knees among the broken shards of clay and splattered soup.

"Eat it," Rowland hissed, raising his foot to push Ilias' face against the planks.

Anik's growl stopped him short. The Lowlander yanked his hand from Ren's grip and drew his sword.

Ren shoved Anik hard in the chest, Anik's back hitting the door frame. His eyes were wide with shock as Ren gripped both his wrists, the tip of Anik's sword scraping the floor. Ren met no resistance. Clearly, Anik hadn't expected Ren to have any fight in him. Slowly, Anik relaxed, and when Ren released his wrists, Anik sheathed his sword.

"I'm sorry you had to see that," Rowland said, sounding genuinely apologetic and offering Ren a sad smile. "The boy can be a handful."

Anik opened his mouth but Ren elbowed him hard in the side to make him close it again.

"It's all right. It's no trouble for us, really. We've been on the road for a while and burnt food is still better than what we've been eating," Ren said, smiling back. He tried to extend that smile to Ilias as well, but the slave's eyes were fixed firmly on his own hands. The boy didn't deserve this. Slowly, Ilias righted himself and began picking up broken shards from the floor. The red mark stood out clearly against his pale cheekbone. The sight made Ren's gut twist.

"Your slave is quick to anger," Rowland noted, looking Anik up and down. "Lowlanders," he continued in a knowing tone. "Am I right?"

Ren swallowed. Any more of this and he wasn't sure he could hold Anik back with a simple elbow in the side. "I haven't had him long."

Ren helped Ilias carry things from the kitchen to the table in an effort to spare the boy any more of Rowland's temper.

Somehow, they managed to make it through dinner without spilling any blood, which Ren considered quite an accomplishment. The meal was delicious; a well-seasoned soup with tender bits of beef, carrot, onion and spice, but Ren was too on edge to enjoy it to the fullest. Anik was a lion ready to close its jaws around Rowland's neck throughout the entire course of the meal, but in the end, they were able to get up and retreat to the guest bedroom upstairs without incident.

Ren dropped his bag brimming with their new purchases by the foot of the bed and sank onto the narrow, hard mattress with a sigh of pleasure. Sleeping under the stars simply didn't live up to the softness of a real bed, even if Rowland's guest bed was only stuffed with hay and not with down like the ones in the castle. The guest room was as dark and uninviting as the rest of Rowland's home and the faint smell of blood hung on the air, but at least it had a roof. Too bad they couldn't spend the night here. Ren's bones and muscles were tired and sore from several days of travel and physical exertion. He ran his hands along his thighs, rubbing at tender muscles.

"He called me a slave," Anik said, voice strange as he leaned against the wall and pushed aside the curtain with a finger to look out onto the street. "Is it really that obvious?"

"Obvious?" Ren asked, but when Anik didn't answer, he shrugged. "It's your accent. The only Lowlanders here are slaves and beggars." Sitting up, he shrugged off his jacket and draped it over a chair, then grabbed a hold of the oil lamp by the side of the bed, striking the flint until a golden glow filled the room.

Anik looked over his shoulder at Ren. His gaze was searching. "So," he said slowly. "It really doesn't faze you, does it?"

"What?" Ren rubbed at the dirty glass of the oil lamp before giving up and placing it back on the night stand.

"Forget it."

"You mean what happened to Ilias?" Ren asked, leaning against the headboard. It creaked ominously against his weight. "Of course it does. You're right. He doesn't seem like he belongs here and Rowland treats him like shit, but I don't think there's anything we-"

"We should free him," Anik said, tone as easy as if he was he talking about buying a chicken at the market.

"Free him? As in break him out?"

"You saw his arms," Anik continued, turning towards Ren and wrapping his own arms over his chest. "That's not weakness. The poor kid was trying to get away from this place. Away from Rowland."

"But we can't steal another man's property," Ren protested.

Before Ren could blink, Anik sprang forward and slammed a fist against the night stand, making the candle topple over and hit the ground, where it broke in two. "Fuck, you are so frustrating! People aren't property," he growled, the anger in his eyes so intense that Ren worried that Anik would draw his sword against him the way he had done in the kitchen, but Anik leaned back and uncurled his fist. He sank to the floor and ran a hand over his hair.

Ren exhaled, letting his racing heart relax.

They were both quiet, trying to determine whether Rowland had heard the noise, Anik's head tilted slightly to the side like a fox listening for a mouse. "He's going to kill that kid," Anik said eventually, voice hushed again. The look in his eyes was raw, almost haunted, and he dropped his hand from his hair to ghost his fingertips over the dip of his throat in a strange gesture.

Ren closed his eyes. Ilias was kind, gentle, soft. Anik had spotted right away that he didn't belong in a place like this, and Ren could see it, too. Ilias would die here.

"All right," Ren said softly, shifting his gaze from Anik to the shadowed doorway. "I'm sorry. You're right." It would be dangerous, reckless, and would jeopardize their entire mission if they were caught. But Ilias couldn't stay here. Imagining Keelan in a place like this made Ren's throat tighten uncomfortably. "So, what's the plan?"

* * *

When Ren and Anik hadn't departed by the time darkness fell, Rowland stuck his head into their room and told them they were welcome to stay until morning, but that they would have to pay extra if they wanted breakfast. Ren thanked him, giving him a pleasant smile. Then they waited until the house went quiet and Rowland put out the light in his bedroom across the narrow hall.

As they sneaked out on silent feet, Ren realized with a pang of worry that Ilias might sleep in Rowland's bed. Luckily, Ren's worry turned out to be unfounded. Rowland must still be angry with Ilias about the incident in the kitchen, because that was where they found him – under a thin blanket on the cold floor. Seeing him now gave Ren a twinge of guilt. The castle hounds in Aleria were treated better, and he had been prepared to leave this place and never look back.

Ilias gasped, eyes wide when they entered, but Anik silenced him with a finger pressed to his lips. Ren's heart sank even further when Ilias stirred, the motion revealing a chain that connected the iron cuffs around his wrists to a ring in the floor.

Anik glanced briefly at the chain. His voice was a whisper. "Don't be afraid. Do you want to leave this place?"

Ilias stared at Anik, then he nodded. He looked like a ghost in the darkness. "More than anything." He spoke so softly that Ren could barely hear him from where he stood by the door.

Anik inspected the chain, and the rattle seemed so loud in the silence that it made Ren cringe.

Ren glanced over his shoulder at the dark staircase that led upstairs.

"Where's the key?" Anik asked Ilias.

The slave pointed to the door. "Master Rowland has it."

Ren took a steeling breath. Leaning against the doorway, he listened for the slightest sound. Everything was quiet, but there was no way they would be able to search Rowland's room for the key without the man waking up.

Anik stood, moving past Ren.

"Where are you going?" Ren hissed, heart beating so hard in his chest he was sure Anik could hear it when he squeezed past him.

"I need something to cut the chain."

Ren was about to protest, but Anik had already slipped past him. Ren watched as he disappeared into Rowland's work room by the front. Every noise made Ren cringe. A few moments later, Anik returned with a bone saw.

"What? No way. It makes too much noise," Ren objected,

staring at the saw as Anik knelt beside Ilias once more.

"I couldn't find a cutter. I'll do it quietly. The chain is thin and I think there's a weak link. It'll be quick."

It wasn't quick. The sound of the saw was like a rasp against the inside of Ren's skull. It was more nerve-wracking than breaking Anik out of the castle dungeon had been. Ren stood in the doorway and felt more exposed than ever.

A creaking sound made Ren's hair stand on end and he motioned frantically for Anik to stop. The sawing paused and they stared at each other in the darkness.

There were footsteps on the stairs.

As quietly as he could, Ren let himself out of the kitchen and closed the door behind him, then slipped out of his sword sheath and his hunting jacket and dropped both on the floor by the bench. He made it to the foot of the stairs just as Rowland came down, and they almost bumped into each other, confusion and suspicion flitting across the large man's features.

"Oh! Rowland, I'm sorry," Ren said, rubbing the back of his neck, movements slow like he had just woken from sleep. "I hope I didn't wake you. I just came down to get something to drink."

"Did you hear that?" Rowland asked slowly, frown deepening.

"Yes, the city noises are odd tonight. I'm having trouble sleeping too." Ren gave him a tired smile and ran his hand through his hair, ruffling it. He watched Rowland's eyes linger there, then on his lips. His own colouring was not far from Ilias', he realised. Pale skin, light hair, blue eyes. He smiled again, more softly this time, chin dipping a little. Looking down, he realised to his dread that he was still wearing his riding boots and he shuffled a little to the side, hoping it was too dark for Rowland to notice. "I'm sorry. I wander when I can't sleep. I'll go back to bed."

Rowland took a step down, closer to Ren. Closer to the kitchen. "It's all right. Let's have a drink together first."

Ren's obfuscation had clearly worked, perhaps a little too well. Rowland's hand was on the staircase railing on the other side of Ren's hip, boxing him in. He could feel the man's breath against the side of his face.

"I shouldn't," Ren said, inching down a step, forcing Rowland to remove his hand when Ren bumped into it. "We're leaving early in the morning. We have a long way to travel."

Rowland chuckled warmly and nodded. "Ah, yes. I know how you young adventurers are. Not satisfied until you've seen the whole world. Well, have a good night then, Niklas. You know where I'll be if you change your mind. Don't worry about waking me," Rowland assured him before turning to walk back up the stairs. Ren didn't relax until he heard the click of the door. The man was foul.

Grabbing his things, he pushed the door to the kitchen open once more, slipping inside. Anik and Ilias had both frozen in place, but relaxed when they saw him. Anik's gaze lingered on

Ren, on his ruffled hair and undershirt.

Flushing, Ren ignored him and dragged his jacket back on, followed by his belt. This wasn't the time to explain himself.

"Help me with the chain," Anik whispered, gesturing to where Ren should hold.

Ren knelt next to the two of them and grabbed the chain with both hands. They tugged hard in opposite directions, the metal creaking slightly. On the third tug, the chain broke apart, the weakened link snapping in two and falling to the floor with a clatter.

They all held their breath and listened. When nothing happened, they rose to their feet, Ren finding a jacket from his bag and wrapping it around Ilias' shoulders, thankful that he had packed more clothes than he really needed. It was a formal jacket, with gold embroidery on the shoulders. People would probably ask questions, but at least he could sell it and buy something less flashy for himself.

They gathered their bags and pulled the kitchen door open. One room and the narrow hallway was all that lay between them and freedom. Ilias followed close behind them, fiddling nervously with his own hands. They were almost in the clear.

Ren would've never expected a man of Rowland's stature to be able to move so quietly.

"What in the world do you think you're doing?" Rowland thundered, shattering the silence. His large form blocked the corridor.

Ren startled, stumbling back into Ilias, who let out a squeak like a frightened mouse.

Reaching back, Ren closed a hand around Ilias' wrist and tugged him back from Rowland just as the man's arm swung out, fist closing on nothing but air.

Anik acted quickly, shoving Rowland hard in the chest with all his strength. Rowland staggered backward, hit the wall, and fell to the floor. Before he could get back up, all three of them leapt over him and fled down the hall.

The door slammed against the wall as Anik shoved it open and they darted out into the yard, through the gate, down the alley, and into the street. Ren's grip on Ilias' wrist was tight, dragging the boy along, but he didn't trip. Behind them, they heard Rowland's angry shouts grow distant. Still, they didn't stop running until their lungs were burning and they had reached the outskirts of the city.

Turning a corner, they leaned against the wall of a building, chests rising and falling heavily. Somehow, they had managed to escape Rowland and avoid whatever guards might still be roaming the city.

Ilias' eyes were wide with shock and excitement. A laugh bubbled up inside Ren and he couldn't help but let it out. Then Anik was laughing too, and then Ilias, until they were all laughing like idiots, alone in an alley in the middle of the night, letting out all the tension that had built up during their daring escape.

They were all right. They had made it.

Ilias' laughter was like bells, his smile radiant, and Ren wondered how long it must have been since he had last laughed like that. His surprised joy reflected Ren's own expression. It was strange to laugh after everything that had happened. A sudden pang of guilt made Ren's smile fade and he blew out a breath. It didn't feel right to laugh like this so soon after his brother's death.

"So, what now?" Ren asked in the silence that followed, looking to Anik.

"I'll fetch the horses," Anik said, dropping his bag at Ren's feet before disappearing around the corner of the building.

"Where are you going?" Ilias asked.

"North," Ren explained, tugging Ilias a little deeper into the shadows when a nearby dog began to bark.

Ilias frowned, cocking his head to the side so that his long hair fell over his shoulder. "Why? What's up there?"

An almost familiar cold slowly seeped back into Ren's bones. He tried to ignore it, but didn't quite manage. "Hope," Ren said simply.

The sound of hooves against stone distracted him from his thoughts, and a moment later, Anik rounded the corner with a horse's reins in each hand. Strapping their bags to the saddles, they mounted, Ren reaching down to help Ilias up behind him.

Anik shook his head. "Not a good idea."

"Why not?" Ren asked, glaring at Anik in confusion. An hour ago, he had been adamant about saving the boy. Now he wanted to leave him behind?

"Where we're going isn't a place for him. We still have days on the road ahead of us, running, hiding, fighting."

"I think your friend is right," Ilias said, smiling at Ren. "You don't have to worry about me. I'll find my own way."

Ren hesitated, ignoring the look Anik gave him when Ilias took his hand and kissed the back of it.

"You saved my life today," Ilias said. "You've already helped me more than I could have ever asked for. I'll be okay, I promise. You go chase that hope."

Ren thought the boy had a surprising amount of confidence, considering his situation. Maybe it was an act, maybe not. Either way, it worked well enough to put Ren at ease.

"Take care of yourself," Anik said, tugging a blanket from his saddlebag. He handed it to Ilias along with their extra water skin and one of their food packets. Ren hesitated, then dug into his money pouch and gave Ilias the few gold coins he had left. There were no more towns between here and Stag's Run. Ilias would need the money more.

"Do you think he'll be okay?" Ren asked when Isleya's faint lights were well behind them. Their horses walked side by side in the tall grass along the road, the thin crescent moon providing the only light.

"He's a Lowlander," Anik said. "He's tougher than he looks."

"Good," Ren said quietly, and then, when Anik shot him a strange look, "What?"

"You're not as much of a heartless ass as I thought," Anik said, although his face betrayed nothing of what he might be feeling.

* * *

The guards didn't follow them. Golden fields stretched out before them, empty and quiet, the horizon broken here and there by clusters of trees that grew more frequent the further from the city they travelled. They rode in silence with only the soft sounds of the horses' steps and the occasional screech of an owl to disturb Ren's thoughts.

The sun rose and travelled across the sky. They ate on horseback, putting as much distance between them and the city as possible. Ren's body ached and he swayed in the saddle from lack of sleep. He kept wondering what Ilias had been doing with that butcher. He had probably been stolen from someone with a whole load of cash, judging by his appearance. Had Ren been back in Aleria, he might have chosen such a slave to serve him his meals. Someone easy on the eyes.

"Hey. Sleepyhead."

Anik's voice disturbed Ren's thoughts and he turned his horse to see the Lowlander dismounting several lengths behind him. Above them, the sky was tinted pink and orange by the setting sun.

"We're staying here for the night."

"Why here?" Ren asked, turning his horse around and dismounting a little unsteadily. He groaned as he stretched out his cramping legs slowly. An entire day and half a night in the saddle with no sleep left its mark. He shook his head to steady his vision, then tied his horse to a nearby tree. Ren felt like he'd never close his legs properly again. And not for any pleasant reason.

"Because you could barely stay upright in the saddle, and because of the river, and because that hill shields us from view from the road," Anik said, pointing to each feature before sinking down on the grass with a sigh. He rolled his shoulders and extended his legs.

At least Ren wasn't the only one feeling spent. It was the first time Anik had shown any real signs of fatigue. They were subtle, like the slightly slower blinks of his eyes and the droop of his shoulders. It was somehow intriguing.

They shared a meal of bread and dried meat. Ren already missed the delicious stew he'd bought in Isleya. Anik didn't get up to catch fish in the river this time. Maybe he was too tired. The apples Keelan had packed for them were starting to go a little

114

soft, but Ren still ate two. It was far removed from the fruits, meats, wines, and sugary treats served in the castle at all hours of the day.

Ren's muscles burned and his sight was blurry, but he knew better than to complain. He was far too tired for another dose of snark from Anik.

A family of boar wandered out into the tall grass between two clusters of trees. Ren watched them bow their heads to turn the soil with their tusks and noses. If he'd had a spear, he could have taken down one of the young ones. Maybe that would have even gained him some respect from Anik. But all he had was his sword, and he couldn't throw that. He watched the boar return to the shelter of the brush, disappearing from Ren's view along with his dream of juicy boar steak.

The constant, endless silence was also hard to tolerate. Anik seemed to prefer it, only speaking to Ren when absolutely necessary, and again, Ren decided not to push.

They finished eating in the same way they had passed the rest of the day – in silence. Ren's entire body screamed for rest as he lay down on his blankets. Anik didn't get up to do his strange training routine this time, but followed Ren's example. Ren fell asleep the moment his eyes slipped closed, but even in sleep, the world seemed keen on denying him a break. His dreams haunted him with memories of his brother, broken and bleeding on the marble floor.

* * *

For once, Ren woke not from the feeling of Anik impatiently shaking him by the shoulder, but because he felt well-rested. Sitting up, he wiped sleep from his eyes and looked around. It was early morning, pheasants calling in the surrounding patches of woodland, a cool fog billowing above the grass. In an hour or two, it'd be burned away by the sun.

A pleasant memory unfolded in his mind, of himself and Hellic camping together in the woods outside Aleria. Thais had been too young to join them, but they hadn't been completely alone. King Callun had sent two guards to watch over them, but Ren could still remember how old and responsible he had felt sleeping outside in the woods and hunting a rabbit with his brother for breakfast. They hadn't skinned it themselves; one of the guards had done that for them. Back then, he'd had no idea how tough it was to travel and sleep under the stars. If Hellic had been here, things would have been different. Ren wouldn't have felt so alone. The space in his heart that Hellic used to occupy still felt glaringly, painfully empty.

Next to him, the spot where Anik had slept was bare. Ren was alone. For a split second, the thought crossed his mind that Anik had abandoned him, but that seemed unlikely. Anik wouldn't have left his bag and his horse, and both were still there.

116

Getting up, Ren stretched and dragged on his boots and his coat, then went off to find Anik.

He didn't have to search long. From the top of the hill, Ren spotted him, standing a distance from their camp, the tall grass reaching up to his thighs. As Ren watched, he swung his sword at an invisible opponent, shifted his balance and changed his grip and thrust the tip of his blade through the air. It wasn't the kind of swordsmanship Ren had been taught. The attacks and blocks were interrupted by those soft, flowing movements that Ren had seen Anik perform a few nights ago.

Ren strode down the hill, stopping a couple yards behind Anik. Anik didn't pause or turn around, although Ren was sure he'd heard him. "What are you doing?"

Anik completed a circular swing of his sword, extending it out from his body before changing his grip and using it to stab in the opposite direction. He was barefoot again, Ren noticed.

"What does it look like?"

Ridiculous slow-dancing with dangerous objects? Ren didn't say that. "What happened to 'we need to get back on the road as fast as possible?'" he asked instead, crossing his arms over his chest.

"We were on the road non-stop for almost twenty hours," Anik said. He thrust the tip of his sword through the air, impaling an invisible enemy. "You haven't unsheathed that fancy, gilded sword of yours yet." Finally, he turned and faced Ren, resting the flat of his sword's blade against his shoulder. "You should train. Get into shape. We'll get back on the road when the sun clears the trees."

"I don't need to train," Ren said with a shrug. "I trained under the royal sword-master for three years."

Anik looked him up and down as though he was trying to determine the value of a cow for slaughter. "And your sword-master didn't teach you about the importance of maintaining your skills?"

Ren bristled. "I can fight. You don't have to worry about me slowing you down."

"Then fight me," Anik said, lowering his sword.

Ren rolled his eyes. "I'm hungry. I want breakfast." He made to turn, but the tip of Anik's sword against the underside of his jaw made him freeze.

"Fight me, skahli," Anik repeated, his eyes boring into Ren's.

"You've got some nerve, asshole," Ren growled, slapping Anik's blade aside with the back of his hand. "What does that word even mean?"

"It's a term of endearment," Anik replied, voice thick with sarcasm.

Ren scowled, spun on his heel and marched back to camp. He found his brother's sword where he'd left it by the side of his blankets and yanked it from its sheath. Maybe just this once, he could put Anik in his place, make the brash, rude Lowlander stop and realise Ren was actually worthy of respect. As he walked back to Anik, Ren tried to remember everything that Berin and the sword-master had taught him about fighting. Proper stance, how to keep balance, the most effective strikes and parries. Anik stood where Ren had left him, waiting with a hand on his hip. Ren would wipe that amused smirk off his face.

Positioning himself in front of Anik in the circle of flattened grass, Ren realised with a hint of trepidation that he had never before sparred against someone else with sharpened blades. He felt confident that he'd be able to keep from injuring Anik. So long as Anik was skilled enough to exercise the same amount of self-control. Ren wanted to see the look of surprise in Anik's eyes when he beat him. Maybe even a bit of admiration. He moved into ready position.

Anik raised his sword, one foot in front of the other, mirroring Ren's stance.

Ren swung.

The impact of steel and against steel was jarring, harder than Ren had anticipated. It ached all the way up his arm as Anik pushed his sword downwards and twisted, forcing Ren to take a step back and break away. Anik's blade sliced through the air, aimed at Ren's throat. Ren raised his blade, parrying just in time to avoid the sharp edge sinking into his flesh. His heart skipped a beat. Anik was serious. Well, Ren could be serious, too.

Anik held his sword at the ready, waiting for Ren to strike.

Ren glanced at Anik's left flank, Anik's arm drawn back to keep balanced. Ren's chance. Stepping in close, Ren feinted to the right and then swung to the left.

Anik didn't take the bait; the force of Anik's blade stopping his strike made Ren stagger. He panted, putting some distance between them. This wasn't what he had expected, not at all. This was like fighting Berin when the older, larger man held nothing back. In contrast to how Ren felt, Anik barely looked like he was exerting himself. Raising his free hand, Anik waved Ren closer. "I said fight me!"

With a snarl, Ren charged. He wanted nothing more than to knock the cocky idiot on his ass and get the upper hand on him for once.

Anik blocked Ren's strikes with frustrating ease. Even in the defence, Ren felt like Anik was only playing with him. Letting Ren drive him back around the ring of grass until-

Steel slid against steel. Ren's arm twisted, pain shooting through the joints. A hard kick against his ankle threw him off balance and he landed hard on his back, nearly slamming his head into the ground.

He had closed his eyes as he landed, and when he opened them again, shining steel gleamed at his throat.

"That's enough," Anik said, stepping back and inspecting the new notches in his blade. The ones in Ren's were deeper.

Ren pushed himself up, rubbing his sore wrist. Anik strode past him up the hill and Ren glared at his back, heat rising to his cheeks, the shame of humiliation mixing with bitter disappointment.

CHAPTER SIX

Anger, disappointment, and shame still curled in Ren's gut as he marched back to the camp and threw his sword on the ground, then changed his mind and picked it back up, sheathing it.

"Where did you learn to fight like that?" Ren demanded, looking Anik up and down.

Anik joined Ren by the burnt-out remnants of the fire, dragged his bag closer and searched through it. "My village," he said. He gave up searching and grabbed the loaf of bread that Ren laid out instead, tearing off a chunk.

"Bullshit," Ren said, staring him down. He snatched the rest of the loaf back from Anik before he could devour it entirely. "Who are you really?"

Anik paused and laughed, the sound muffled by all the bread

he had stuffed in his mouth. He swallowed. "What, you think I must be some secret, powerful warrior prince of a mysterious, faraway nation for me to be able to beat you at sticks?" Anik smiled mockingly and shook his head, washing down the bread with water. "Maybe you should consider that you're just too far up your own ass to want to believe you just got it handed to you by a simple farm boy."

Ren felt his face grow red and he opened his mouth to serve Anik a piece of his mind, but Anik cut him off.

"Here's the difference, skahli," Anik continued, leaning forward on his elbows. "You trained because it was a formality. Because it was a fancy skill to have, so you could parade around dinner parties with a shiny golden blade strapped to your hip and tell everyone you know how to use it. Where I come from, we train for survival, because if we didn't, we'd end up with our heads severed and mounted on sticks outside our village. That's why you'll never be as good as I am."

Anik stood, grabbing his blankets and rolling them up before swinging his bag over his shoulder.

Ren remained by the fire with a dry loaf of bread in his hands, red-faced and feeling like an idiot as he watched Anik go to the horses. Any semblance of camaraderie developed between them in Isleya seemed to have vanished with the morning fog. Ren should have expected as much. He knew Anik was a cold and unsympathetic dick.

Still, Ren couldn't help but consider what Anik had said as he stood and folded up his blankets, packing them away in his bag. As little as he liked to admit it, Anik was right. Ren had trained half-heartedly, knowing that he would never truly need to fight. That had been Hellic's job. Hellic, the crown prince, the beacon of hope for every soldier. Neither of them had ever seen a real battle, but Hellic had still been far superior to Ren on the training field. Hellic had been dedicated and hard-working, while Ren had been too busy chasing youths to care.

Ren worked to swallow the lump in his throat that seemed to have lodged itself there since his brother's death. He stuffed the blankets into his bag with too much force. It had been his job to protect his younger brother. He had failed.

A sound like a yelp made Ren straighten up and look around. The horses were tacked, but Anik was nowhere to be seen. Swearing under his breath, Ren swung his bag over his shoulder and scaled the hill at a run, grip tight on the hilt of his sword.

Anik stood at the bottom of the hill, but this time, he wasn't alone. The tip of his sword hovered at a stranger's throat in the same way he had challenged Ren that morning.

"What did you do to him?" the stranger hissed, loud enough for Ren to hear. He drew a short dagger from his belt.

Ren's breath hitched. He knew that voice.

Anik moved forward, his sword dangerously close to the newcomer's throat.

"Stop!" Ren shouted, descending the hill towards them, boots slipping against the dewy grass.

The stranger turned sharply, almost dropping his dagger at the sight of Ren. "Ren!" he called, voice cracking with emotion as he fumbled to sheathe his dagger and yank back the hood that cast his face into shadow. A moment later, Niklas' body slammed into Ren's own as he wrapped his arms around Ren in a crushing hug. "I was so afraid you were dead," Niklas croaked, looking Ren up and down to make sure he wasn't hurt.

"I'm fine. Anik can be trusted," Ren assured him, even if it stung a little to admit. Anik might be an ass, but at least the Lowlander hadn't betrayed him yet. Anik stood behind Niklas, his sword back in its sheath, although his expression remained wary.

"What are you doing here? Did something happen?" Ren asked, worry suddenly replacing the relief he had felt at seeing Niklas' familiar face. He stepped back, but let Niklas hold onto his hand.

"I want to come with you," Niklas said firmly. He tightened his grip.

"Tell me everything," Ren said.

They walked back over the hill, Anik at the back, Niklas with an arm slung over Ren's shoulder.

"Things are getting worse back home. Halvard executed two of our generals in the courtyard. People were talking about hostages and war and I panicked. I couldn't stay there."

"Fuck." A hard ball of ice formed in Ren's gut at Niklas' words. "How did you get here? I don't suppose you walked."

Niklas flushed and shook his head. "No, I had a horse, but I lost it last night, bags and all. Fucking idiotic; I must not have secured it well enough. I had just about given up trying to find you when I went to get water from the river and stumbled upon your guard dog," he said, gesturing over his shoulder at Anik.

"What about Thais?" Ren asked. A part of him wished Niklas had stayed in the castle where he could have watched over his brother, but a more selfish part of him was grateful at the prospect of having a friend along on the journey. Anik certainly didn't count.

"I don't know anything new." Niklas' expression was apologetic. "I left only a day after you did. As far as I know, they still have him locked up."

Ren sighed, putting his bag down by the ashes of the campfire and digging through it. "Here, you should eat," he said, handing Niklas some of the dried bread and meat. "We'll wait for you."

Ren almost expected Anik to protest and hurry them on, but he stayed quiet. Instead, he left them to return to the horses. He was meticulous, checking their hooves one by one and adjusting the saddles as if looking for any excuse not to spend time in their company.

"Why are you still travelling with him?" Niklas asked. He watched Anik too, but when he bit into the dry loaf of bread, he grimaced at it like it had personally offended him. Ren resisted a smile. He was glad to see he wasn't the only one finding the countryside cuisine subpar.

"He knows the way," Ren said with a shrug. "And he fights well. It's kind of like having a hired guard you don't have to pay."

"A guard who might murder you in your sleep. How convenient." Niklas didn't sound impressed.

"He wants Halvard dead. The enemy of my enemy is my friend, and all that," Ren said, then winced. 'Friend' was far-fetched.

"Uh-huh," Niklas said, swallowing hard against the dry bread. "Is that what he told you?"

"You don't like him, do you?"

"Don't tell me you do." Niklas' mouth twisted.

Ren huffed. "Not at all. Believe me, you'll like him even less in a few days." Reaching for the water skin, he took a drink of the cool water they had gathered from the river before passing it to Niklas. "He finds flaws in every part of me. My skills, my fighting style, my personality, my opinions. Even my flaws have flaws, apparently."

"What a total dickhead."

Ren hummed in agreement.

"You took out your earrings," Niklas noted. "It's weird to see you without them."

Ren raised his hand and felt along his bare earlobe. "It's safer this way."

"You're right," Niklas said, reaching up to touch his own single gold stud, then slipped it out and pocketed it. "I'd value not losing my head over being mistaken for a commoner," he said with a small laugh.

Ren smiled. It was as if Niklas presence alone was lifted his and increased his energy. Watching his friend brush crumbs from his hands, Ren stood up.

"Let's move out, farmer boy," Ren barked at Anik, which earned him a grin of approval from Niklas.

* * *

After so many days in near silence, having Niklas with them was almost overwhelming. Sitting behind Ren on his horse, hands clasped lightly around his waist, Niklas hardly stopped talking for more than a few seconds at a time. At first, he was clearly cautious, avoided talking about their home or the castle or Ren's family, but when Ren didn't object, Niklas began to relax. They talked about everything from dancing to horses to embarrassing childhood stories, like the time King Callun had tripped over his night pot in the darkness, or when Thais got his head stuck between the metal bars of the garden gates as a toddler. It was as if they'd been apart for months and not days.

They talked about Hellic, too – how much he had loved the

128

prize mare Ren had bought him for his fifteenth birthday, and the time they had tried to throw apples over the castle spires and Hellic had accidentally tossed an apple through his father's open window, hitting him in the back of the head during an important business meeting.

Talking about Hellic was cathartic. It felt good to replace the thoughts of him bleeding out on the marble floor with better, happier memories. Ren found he could smile, even laugh at the dramatic way Niklas retold their stories.

As usual, Anik rode ahead of them, not sparing them either a glance or a word. Ren didn't care. Anik could do as he liked.

They stopped a few hours earlier than usual to make camp for the night. Anik said Ren's horse would need extra rest now that it had to carry two people instead of one. He also complained about the extra mouth to feed and noted that their food rations wouldn't stretch as far, especially now that it would be getting colder and they would need all the energy they could get.

Ren couldn't find it in him to be bothered by Anik's hard tone now that Niklas was with him. Niklas' presence soothed Ren's temper. They had been best friends for as long as Ren could remember, had been raised together. Niklas was one year older than Ren, and the son of a powerful Skarlan lord. Orphaned early in life, infant Niklas had been gifted to the court of Frayne from Skarlan as a sign of peace, along with the three big cats that Ren's family kept in the dungeons. In exchange, Ren's mother, the queen, then princess of Frayne, had visited the Skarlan capital of Iskaal to relay Frayne's appreciation of the truce, along with a gift of five pure-bred Fraynean horses.

It was there, away from the supervision of her parents, that the princess had lain with a slave, and nine months later given birth to Ren. Ren didn't like to think about that part of the story. When he was young, the other children would tease him about it, call him half a slave with dirty blood. They said his father was a Lowlander, and would try to prove it by taunting him into starting a fight. Ren had always resisted. He had grown up handsome, elegant, and graceful, and he was thankful for that, even if his light head of hair made him stand out from the rest of his family. Maybe that was why he and Niklas had always gotten along so well – they shared the burden of a distrusted heritage. At least Ren had been able to shake most of that reputation as he grew older and made a good name for himself in court. Niklas had never been quite so lucky.

They ate, tended to the horses, and stretched out, tired after two days of constant riding. Ren laid out his blankets and Niklas rolled up in them and fell asleep almost at once.

Despite his silence, Anik's mood seemed to have improved. He hummed a quiet tune to himself as he smoothed out his blankets and then grabbed his sword. Loneliness must be as cathartic to him as company was to Ren, as odd as it seemed.

Sunset was still over an hour away and Ren wasn't tired, so

when Anik wandered off to practice, Ren followed him to watch. It was the same style Anik always used, slow and focused. Precise. He had taken off his shirt and Ren was close enough to see his ribcage expand and contract, seemingly to the same rhythm as his steps. Had Ren not known that the man performing this strange, serene sword-dance was such an asshole, he would have found it beautiful.

As Ren watched him, he couldn't help the nagging feeling growing in his gut. That feeling of inferiority and lacking he could admit to himself, but to Anik? Surely, he could stand Anik's mocking glares if it meant he wouldn't die at the hand of a Skarlan soldier. Like with any exchange, you had to be able to put up with a certain level of discomfort to get what you wanted. Ren had done it so many times before.

Bracing himself, Ren stood. "Is that dancing thing what makes you so good at fighting?" he asked as he approached, head tilted slightly.

Anik turned slowly, lowering his arms. He looked Ren over. "Part of it."

Ren looked at the scar on Anik's shoulder, then further down at his tattoos. Anik saw him staring but said nothing.

"Can you teach me?" Ren asked, searching Anik's expression. He wasn't scowling, instead regarding him with a furrowed brow as if what Ren had asked didn't quite make sense. Maybe Ren really had caught him in a rare good mood, or maybe he had simply surprised him.

"Why?" Anik asked warily.

"You said it yourself," Ren said with a casual shrug. "I'm bad at fighting. I don't want to have to rely on you to save my ass if it comes to that, so I might as well train. And your way seems to be the best way."

The furrow between Anik's brows deepened, his lips parting in subtle confusion. Ren wasn't sure if his request counted as surrender or not, but at least he got the satisfaction of surprising the grouchy Lowlander for once.

"I can't teach you something like this in a few days. It takes months, maybe even years to learn. You're better off working on what you already know how to do," Anik said, taking a step back.

Ren raised an eyebrow. "Is there really something Anik, the great warrior, can't do?" he teased. "I'm shocked."

Anik dropped his head and shook it, and Ren thought he saw the slightest hint of a smile tug at the corner of his mouth before he placed his sword down on the grass and straightened up. "All right then, castle boy. Take off your boots."

Going barefoot felt odd. Based on Anik's explanation, it had something to do with being connected to the earth. Ren wasn't sure he felt connected to anything as he lifted one foot off the ground, wobbled, and took a large, awkward step forward to keep from falling. He felt ridiculous. He most likely looked ridiculous, too.

Anik looked graceful and strong as he demonstrated the motions and positions beside him, but Ren honestly wasn't sure what this exercise had to do with getting better at sword fighting. He felt like a drunk, one-legged goose, and he kept forgetting to breathe in that strange way Anik insisted he should.

Anik nudged him in the back, urging him to straighten up, widen his stance, move more confidently, all while training Ren with that icy glare of disapproval that sometimes mixed with amusement when Ren made a fool of himself. After twenty minutes, Ren was sweating like a pig. It was surprising how taxing it could be to move so slowly. Next to him, Anik looked like he had barely exerted himself at all, loose-limbed and calm, his cheeks flushed like he had just woken up from a pleasant nap.

"I thought this was supposed to make me better at sword fighting," Ren said, glancing at their untouched weapons as he stole a moment to rest, hands braced on his thighs.

"You have to crawl before you can walk. I told you, you're better off sticking to what you know." Anik leaned his naked back against a tree, watching Ren brush his sweat-damp hair back from his forehead. Ren got the distinct feeling that Anik had only indulged him in the first place so he could watch him make a complete fool of himself.

But Anik's expression wasn't mocking. It wasn't even displeased. Maybe he really was in a good mood. With Anik, it was always hard to tell. To Ren's relief, Anik didn't make to

133

continue the training and Ren took it as his cue to relax.

"Really," Ren began. He sat down on the grass, stretching out his legs. He winced when the tendons along the undersides of his knees burned. "Where did you learn this?" He looked up at Anik, but the Lowlander wasn't looking at him, but at the distant treeline. Ren knew he was watching for danger. Anik's hand came up, fingertips stroking ever so lightly over the dip of his throat like he was fiddling with an invisible necklace. Ren had seen him do it once before, but wasn't sure what it meant. The silence stretched on and Ren almost gave up on receiving an answer, but then Anik spoke again.

"The village blacksmith taught me."

Ren blinked. "No."

"Yes," Anik said, meeting his eyes, one corner of his lip curling upwards.

"So the blacksmith is the secret, powerful warrior prince of a mysterious, faraway nation," Ren said, unable to help himself. He threw up his hands in a grand gesture, like he had figured it all out.

Anik's head dipped, shoulders shaking. The motion was followed by a sound that made Ren gawk: light, rippling laughter. Not a sarcastic grin triggered by Ren's ignorance or in mockery of his flaws, but sincere, light-hearted laughter than creased the corners of Anik's eyes. Ren had heard it once before, after their daring escape from Rowland the butcher, but then it

134

had been mixed with the sounds of his own and Ilias' voices. Now he could hear it clearly and it was strange. It was easy to forget that Anik was even capable of laughter.

Their eyes met and Anik's gaze flickered before he turned his head away and silence fell over them once more. Anik folded his arms over his chest like he was protecting himself from the cold. The temperatures were starting to get lower at night, and he wasn't wearing a shirt.

Footsteps broke the silence and Ren looked up to see Niklas approaching from the camp, woken from his sleep. His gaze lingered on Anik and grew dark. "What are you doing? Sneaking off to fuck in the bushes?" Niklas asked, voice dry as he shot Ren a surprisingly accusing look.

"Don't be stupid," Ren said, pushing himself up. "We were training."

Niklas shot a long glance at their untouched swords on the ground. "Yeah, I can see that."

Ren felt his cheeks burning, even though Niklas' accusation couldn't have been further from the truth. "Seriously," he said, in an attempt to change the subject. He picked up his blade. "You should train, too. I don't want you to get skewered by a guard's sword."

"It's too late for that now," Niklas said, suppressing a yawn. "Besides, I don't-"

A new sound made them all freeze: deep, rasping barks

interrupted by the baying howls of hunting dogs in the distance.

Anik moved first. Grabbing his discarded sword, he darted back to the camp. His sharp voice startled Ren out of his frozen state. "We're downwind! Get the horses!"

Ren turned, fetched his sword and raced for the horses. The animals tossed their heads nervously. Fumbling in the half-darkness, Ren tugged the girths tight. Niklas ran towards him, taking both horses by the reins.

Word of their escape had travelled faster than Ren had thought.

"Maybe it's just a boar-hunting party?" Niklas asked tensely, looking over his shoulder in direction of the sounds. They were getting louder.

Anik joined them and tossed Ren's bag to him before leaping into his own saddle and taking the reins from Niklas. "In the middle of an open field after sunset? I doubt it," he said, circling his horse impatiently as he waited for Ren and Niklas to mount up. He held the reins loosely in one hand, his sword in the other.

As Ren helped Niklas up behind him, the sound of countless hooves against the hard ground mixed with the voices of the dogs.

"Towards the trees," Anik shouted, pulling his horse around. It burst into a gallop from a standstill and Ren spun his own horse to follow. Niklas' arms were tight around his waist as they raced through the tall grass. The sound of the dogs grew fainter, but the thunder of hooves didn't lessen. A large, flat meadow lay between them and the treeline, and Ren heard shouts and barked orders. They were exposed and vulnerable in the open.

Twisting in the saddle, Ren dared a look over his shoulder. Over the hill came six pursuers. They weren't Fraynean castle guards, bearing instead the grey uniforms of the Skarlan forces. Even in the half-darkness, Ren could see the shine of their brandished swords. Shit. How had the Skarlans found them so fast?

They cleared a narrow stream, water splashing Ren's trousers.

Ren's horse was lagging. Carrying two people, it trailed Anik's mount by almost seven lengths. Behind them, their followers closed in. Ren dug his heels into the horse's sides, but the animal was already panting from exertion. The treeline drew closer and closer, but it wouldn't be enough. They weren't fast enough.

Anik reined his horse in, the mare tossing her head and struggling against the bit with the desire to go faster. Like Ren, Anik knew they weren't going to make it – Ren could see it in his eyes when he turned in the saddle.

Ren drew his sword.

Then disaster struck. Fatigued, Ren's horse tripped.

Ren yanked the reins and the horse stumbled again, trying to regain its balance. It huffed in fear before slamming chest-first into the ground. Ren felt himself fly from the saddle, shoulder hitting the ground hard before Niklas landed on top of him. Ren groaned, struggling to free himself, desperate to check for broken bones. No sharp pains shot through his body as he pushed himself to his hands and knees. He looked around, eyes wide in the darkness. Next to him, Niklas groaned and sat up, cradling his left arm.

The first arrow thumped into the ground to Ren's left and he flinched, scrambling away from it as he reached for his sword. So this was how King Halvard would tell the tale: the bastard prince fled like a dog, surrounded by brave men on an open field and shot down by half a dozen arrows in his cowardly attempt to save his own life.

Ren's head spun from the fall. There were horses all around them, so close Ren could feel the impacts of their hooves shake the ground. Anik had been right about him. He had never fought a man to the death.

A second arrow struck, but it didn't bury itself in Ren's heart as he had half-anticipated. Instead, the still-vibrating arrow was embedded at the feet of the nearest Skarlan's horse. The creature whinnied, dancing backward as more arrows followed the first. Three more arrows all found their marks in the bodies of the Skarlan riders.

Scrambling to his feet, Ren looked around wildly. From the darkness of the trees came a single rider on a horse with no saddle. Her long hair whipped around her head as she swung a curved blade and buried it in the chest of a Skarlan soldier.

Another fell to an arrow like the three others, archers appearing from between the trees. Ren spun around, searching for the last Skarlan soldier, but he had already dropped to the ground. Face split in two, the man lay at the feet of Anik's horse.

Relief flooded Ren's system despite the ache in his body. They were alive.

The strangers approached, regarding them in the half darkness. Ren met the eyes of a few of them and felt a bit of his relief fade. They weren't guards, nor villagers or soldiers. They didn't look like any Frayneans Ren had ever seen. Next to him, Niklas groaned again and Ren reached down to help him to his feet without taking his eyes off the strangers.

Of the six newcomers, four were women and two men, all six dressed in worn clothing. Their faces were hard as they scattered to gather the horses that hadn't fled as well as the arrows they had used to slaughter the soldiers. Ren felt Niklas' hand close around his wrist.

One of their rescuers, a dark-skinned woman with hair down to her waist, drew her weapon and approached Ren's fallen horse. It was still breathing, but lay still on its side. As Ren watched, she raised her blade and placed the tip of it against the place where the horse's neck met its head. Ren looked away. That horse had served him well, both here and back in Aleria. Several of the strangers regarded him with searching glances and Ren forced himself to school his expression.

The woman stood, wiping her sword on the chest of a fallen soldier, then turned her attention towards Ren. She looked him up and down, before turning to the woman on the horse, the only rider among them. Foreign words flowed in a soft, song-like rhythm.

It wasn't the woman who answered, but Anik. He spoke in the same language, his voice sounding somehow different when it was coloured by the strange, foreign tones.

Ren gawked. He knew the Lowlands had their own language, but as far as he knew, it had long since disappeared.

"What's going on?" Niklas whispered, body tense and straight as a rod where he stood pressed against Ren's side.

"I don't know," Ren replied.

A brief moment of silence followed Anik's words. Swallowing, Ren squared his shoulders and directed his words to the woman on the horse, who he assumed was the leader, giving her a friendly smile. "Thank you for your help. You saved our lives." He glanced briefly at Anik, but Anik's expression was impossible to read.

To Ren's relief, the woman grinned, patting her horse on the shoulder. "Always happy to cut down Skarlan scum," she replied, her accent thicker than Anik's, though not unpleasant. Whatever Anik had said to them, it at least hadn't made their situation worse.

Next to him, Niklas shifted, and Ren turned to see him

clutching his arm. His sleeve was torn and the skin stained red.

Ren bit his lip. "You're bleeding."

"It's just a cut. I think I scraped my arm on some rocks when we fell," Niklas said, although he had paled considerably.

"You should come with us," the woman on the horse offered, riding up to the two of them. She leaned down, eyes trained on Niklas' arm. "We have a camp nearby. You can rest and bind the wound before you move on."

Ren extended his hand to her. "Thank you. That's very kind. I'm...Berin," he said, and widened his smile. "This is Niklas and Anik."

"Sifa," she said, giving his hand a brief but firm shake. "And it's no trouble. Us little people gotta stick together."

"Absolutely."

She straightened and led the way on horseback towards the trees, waving a hand in the air.

Picking his bag up from the ground, Ren followed, Niklas close behind. Meeting Anik's eyes, he shot Ren a pointed glare, one eyebrow raised. Ren decided to ignore it.

Sifa led them through the undergrowth to a well-hidden clearing, the surrounding brush so dense that the fire lighting up the surroundings couldn't be seen from the outside. Several heads raised when they approached, then bowed to Sifa in respectful greeting. The camp housed eight people in total, all of them Lowlanders. It had been difficult to see in the darkness, but by

141

the light of the fire, black ink stood out clearly against patches of exposed skin, the lines and swirls similar to the ones Anik bore.

The Lowlanders crowded around Anik the moment he dismounted and spoke to him both in the common language and their own. Ren listened to him patiently answering all their questions and asking some of his own. Ren didn't interfere. He had never been surrounded by this many Lowlanders before in his life, and he hadn't imagined it ever happening without a knife buried in his gut. They weren't all as intimidating as Anik had been when Ren had approached him in the cells, but the woman who had killed Ren's horse kept shooting him glares that sent shivers down his spine.

The Lowlanders smiled and welcomed them to their camp and offered them places by the fire, but Ren couldn't help but think their hospitality would only last until they figured out who he really was. Despite it, Anik seemed to sense no danger, or perhaps he didn't care about the risk to Ren's life. These were his people, and they spoke like old friends even though Anik told Ren he had never met them before.

Ren sat down and extended his hands towards the flames. He tried not to think about his dead horse laying out in the field. Crows, foxes and wolves would have a feast tonight.

Niklas' cut had stopped bleeding but his pallor hadn't improved, and Ren suspected it didn't just have to do with his injury. Niklas jumped when one of the Lowlanders placed a hand on his shoulder to guide him towards a seat on a fallen log. If the refugees noticed his discomfort, they didn't seem to mind.

A young man with light brown hair and pretty blue eyes sat down next to Niklas with a bowl of water and a cloth. Carefully, he peeled back the sleeve of Niklas' jacket and washed the cut. The young man's tattoo was small, circling only his wrist, the pattern unrecognisable as anything specific, although Ren assumed they all meant something. On the side of the youth's neck was a brand, a circular symbol with an angular S inside it.

"You're work slaves," Ren said.

Sifa made a sound of displeasure, coming to sit on the log next to Ren. "Former slaves," she corrected. "We fled Skarlan just over a month ago."

"Well, you're on the wrong side of Skarlan if you're trying to get home," Ren said.

Sifa leaned forward, stoking the fire with a stick. "It's easier to survive here than in Skarlan," she explained. "King Halvard has claimed the Lowlands as his property. He'd catch us again if we returned. Thankfully, the Fraynean king is lazy. He hides behind his high walls and drinks wine and feasts on suckling pigs. He doesn't care what the peasants are doing. Bad for the people who live here, but good for us," she said with a shrug.

Ren clenched his jaw, resisting the urge to get up and leave. He longed to tell Sifa that she was wrong, that she didn't understand what it took to protect a country and be a good king.

Callun had worked harder for Frayne than anyone Ren had ever known.

"So, what, you're making your home here?" Ren asked instead and looked around.

Sifa shook her head. "Not here. This is temporary. We've been on the road for a while, but heard these Skarlans were in the area, so we decided to wait and see if they would come our way. They did," she said, sharing a grin with one of the others. Ren recognized her as an archer.

Ren glanced at Anik, but Anik wasn't paying attention to them. Despite having been chased across open fields by angry Skarlan soldiers, Anik seemed comfortable and relaxed, engaged in conversation with one of the refugees in their own, strange language. As Ren watched, the two of them laughed quietly, and he wondered if they were mocking his family, too. He wondered what these people would do if they found out he had been eating suckling pig with the Fraynean king all his life.

Suddenly, Anik raised his head and their eyes met. The smile Anik gave Ren was unlike any Ren had seen from him so far. It was happy and relaxed and lasted only a second before they both looked away.

"What are you doing here?" Sifa asked, angling her head at Ren.

Ren's eyes returned to her. "Running from the Skarlans, same as you," he said. "They've been moving farther and farther across the border. We didn't want to stick around when they came to burn down our town."

Sifa hummed, then gestured with both hands for everyone to gather around. One of the men stood, disappearing into the darkness and reappearing a moment later, carrying a wooden keg over one shoulder. Sifa filled bowls with its rich, golden contents and passed them around as the Lowlanders introduced themselves. Ren remembered none of the foreign-sounding names, except Leine, which was the name of the dark-skinned woman who had killed his horse. As far as he understood, she was Sifa's second.

"What is this?" Niklas asked, suspiciously sniffing the contents of his own bowl. He was still pale, but no longer looked like he was seconds from fainting.

It was Sifa who answered. "It's kalg, a Skarlan drink. The soldiers we killed last week had two kegs on a wagon," she said, and laughed, emptying her bowl in one go before refilling it.

Ren lifted his bowl, sniffed it, and took a sip. It was hard not to grimace. The taste was nothing like wine. It was sharp, with an aftertaste not unlike blood. It sent a wave of heat all the way down his throat and into his chest.

A young woman next to him grinned and refilled his bowl. "Drink some more, that'll make it taste better."

Ren didn't think it was a particularly good idea to get drunk while on the run from people who wanted to kill them. They had

145

to keep moving, stay focused on the mission. He had made a habit of never drinking enough to lose his inhibitions in public. It clouded his mind and made him careless. In Aleria, he had quickly discovered that making deals drunk was the worst thing he could do, especially when those deals involved physical favours.

Still, that didn't stop him from emptying his bowl a second time and holding it out for another refill. The strong kalg made everything seem a little less grim, death not as final, their journey not as desperate. It made it easier not to think about Callun and Hellic and their slit throats, the generals' executions, and Thais controlled by King Halvard on his family's throne. He wouldn't get drunk, but he deserved to relax a little.

"How's your arm?" Ren asked when Niklas came over to sit beside him. It had been neatly wrapped with white linen.

"Feels all right," Niklas said, testing it by turning his arm slowly. Then he gestured to the Lowlanders. "Pretty unsettling, huh?"

"Well, they haven't tried to kill us yet," Ren said.

"You should get rid of him now."

"Hmm?" Ren looked across at Niklas, the light from the fire giving his friend's green eyes and curly hair a golden hue.

Niklas wasn't looking at him, but at Anik. "These are his people. I'm sure he wouldn't mind staying with them." Niklas returned his gaze to Ren.

"I still need his help."

"We can figure it out on our own," Niklas argued. "We just need to know which way is north. Stag's Run is so close, now."

Ren shook his head. "There isn't time to experiment. We need to know exactly where we're going."

"You don't know if he killed your family – killed Hellic."

Ren's mind struggled to keep up with the conversation. The mention of Hellic brought with it memories that Ren didn't want to think about. "I don't think he did, Niklas. I don't want to talk about this." He stood.

Niklas gripped his wrist and gave him a pointed look. "Don't drink any more of that kalg. You're going to be drunk off your ass."

"Yeah, yeah," Ren said, for once wishing Niklas would just leave him alone.

"Ren. I'm serious."

Ren tugged his hand from Niklas' grip.

Someone grabbed Ren by the wrist and tugged him towards the edge of the clearing. A game was being set up. Ren wasn't sure what the rules were, but he played anyway. It had something to do with knocking sticks down in a certain order by throwing rocks at them. Ren was terrible at it. Everybody laughed. Anik laughed, too. His eyes glowed golden in the light of the fire, creased at the corners, sharp canines revealed by his smile. He was even more handsome when he smiled.

147

"Niklas, you try. I don't want to be the worst one at this," Ren said, looking around to find his friend, but Ren couldn't spot him. Instead, he left the line of throwers and passed his rocks to a young girl with a blonde braid so long she could almost wrap it around her waist as a belt.

He sat on a log next to Anik, regarding him. He wasn't bad-looking, really. Not at all. Maybe if he hadn't been a total asshole, and if their situation had been different, Ren would have tried to charm him into bed. Maybe. He was still a Lowlander, after all. But then again, so was Ilias, and his beauty had rivalled any of the slaves in Aleria.

Sifa joined them with three new bowls of kalg. Someone had opened the second keg, although, in their defence, the first one had been almost empty when they started. She offered Anik a bowl, but he held up a hand in polite refusal. Ren took one and downed its contents in one gulp. The girl had been right – it really didn't taste that bad anymore.

Sifa laughed heartily and followed Ren's example, then tossed her bowl over her shoulder and handed the last one to Ren. Standing, she locked her arms around Leine's waist and the two of them started dancing to the rhythm of the spectators' claps.

"Whoa there," Anik said, tugging Ren's bowl from his hands as he was about to raise it to his lips. "You have to be able to ride a horse tomorrow."

"I'm not drunk," Ren argued with a frown, resting his elbows on his knees. The world spun a little, like he was standing on the deck of a ship, but that was all. Really. "Besides, my horse is dead. One horse is not enough for three people."

"All the more reason to stop now," Anik said, setting Ren's bowl out of reach. "I'll talk to Sifa and Leine in the morning, maybe figure out a deal for the horses they took from the soldiers."

"Fine," Ren said. He didn't feel like arguing. He narrowed his eyes at Anik. The man hardly looked like he had been drinking except for a slight flush to his cheeks that could just as well be the heat from the fire.

"What?" Anik asked, raising an eyebrow at the way Ren was watching him.

Ren wanted to tell him that he was really much too handsome to be such an unpleasant grump all the time, but an uncomfortable buzz in his fingertips distracted him. It travelled slowly up his arms to his elbows and grew in intensity. Anik said something to him, the words unintelligible and Ren raised his head with a frown.

"What?"

Anik spoke again, but the words that left his mouth made no sense, as if Anik was speaking the Lowlander language again, although Ren knew he wasn't. Ren narrowed his eyes. His throat was buzzing now, too. He tried to swallow and found he couldn't. Anik was looking at him with concern.

Cries and shouts filled the camp. Ren turned his head towards the sounds, body swaying slightly. It was difficult to focus his vision, but by the light of the fire, Ren could see a figure collapsed on the ground. It was Sifa. Her eyes rolled back in her head.

Ren felt hands grip his shoulders tight. Someone shouted close by and then the world tipped and everything turned black.

CHAPTER SEVEN

Voices.

Rough blankets against his skin.

The touch of a hand against his brow felt like burning metal.

Ren groaned and turned his head away. Even that seemed like an effort, an immense demand of energy.

His body was on fire, but he was trembling with cold.

Someone spoke to him, said his name. Anik. Niklas. A stranger. He couldn't say anything in reply, his mind floating somewhere above his body. He breathed out splinters of wood and metal that rasped his throat raw when he tried to speak. The earth shook with tremors that lasted far too long to be an earthquake, until he realised it wasn't the ground but his body that was shaking.

Minutes passed like days, and all Ren could focus on was how much he wanted it to stop.

The first time he opened his eyes, he was alone. He wanted to scream, to cry out. He was on a cot, covered in blankets, shielded from the outside world by the canvas flaps of a makeshift tent. His stomach roiled when he tried to move and he fought to swallow it down. He squeezed his eyes shut.

The second time he opened his eyes, Niklas was there. He held Ren's hand in a too-firm grip, his head bowed and his shoulders shaking. Ren tried to speak, to tell him not to cry, and judging by Niklas' startled reaction, he had at least succeeded in making a sound.

"You're awake! Fuck, I was so scared you were going to die. How are you feeling?" Niklas asked, wiping at his eyes with the back of a hand.

Groaning, Ren furrowed his brows and closed his eyes. Niklas was speaking much too quickly, his voice too loud. It felt like Ren's body and mind were wrapped in a blanket of stinging thorns.

"What happened?" Ren asked, voice rasping and rough.

"You've been poisoned," Niklas answered, the dread in his voice the last thing Ren heard before he slipped back into the darkness.

His mind was ravaged by fever dreams, shapes and shadows dancing over his floating body; dark, angry creatures. They screamed at him, screamed so loudly he thought his ears might

152

start to bleed.

The third time Ren opened his eyes, strong hands were yanking him upright. A stern voice commanded him to stand, and he tried before realizing his legs wouldn't hold him and he collapsed. The hands caught him, holding him against a firm chest. He wanted to fall back asleep there, but the hands wouldn't let him. Neither would the voice, loud and insistent in his ear.

"Ren! Ren, for fuck's sake, wake up. We have to go." It was Anik's voice, and he sounded angry – not that that was anything new. "You have to walk, Ren. Focus!"

Ren tried. He really did. Swallowing, he found that his throat felt like cotton. He willed his legs to straighten so he could take a step. One, then another.

"Hurry up!" Another voice. Niklas.

What was happening?

Anik pushed the tent flat aside and Ren made a sound of discomfort, squinting in the too-bright daylight. What time was it? What day was it?

Anik mercilessly dragged him along, Ren's feet skidding along the dew-wet grass. He tripped and fell. Anik caught him and hauled him back up.

There were other voices, too, angry voices. Angrier than Anik's. Ren struggled to piece together what had happened while his heart hammered with the effort to stay upright, to keep moving forward. He gulped in lungfuls of fresh air that helped

153

clear his mind of a bit of the haze.

The Lowlander refugee camp. The drinking. Their leader, Sifa, collapsing at the same time as Ren did. Niklas had said he had been poisoned…then so had she. Ren couldn't get it to make sense.

They reached an open field. The wheat was cut short already, leaving only the severed stems.

"Take him," Anik shouted, dumping all Ren's weight on Niklas, who groaned. Ren didn't see where Anik went, keeping his eyes trained on the path ahead. Niklas struggled to support both his weight and that of their bags. Ren could feel him trembling from exertion and he wanted to help him, but even raising his arm to steady himself against Niklas' shoulder felt like a monumental task.

Then Anik was back at his side, slipping an arm around Ren's back to take his weight. Looking down, he saw that Anik had drawn his sword. The blade was red with blood.

When Ren looked back up, they were surrounded by trees. His vision narrowed, darkened at the edges. He stumbled over rocks and tree roots and he reached up to clasp a tight hand around the back of Anik's neck to steady himself.

"He's going to pass out. We need to stop," Niklas said, panting almost as hard as Ren.

"If they catch us, they'll kill us," Anik hissed back, dragging Ren mercilessly onwards.

After another hundred yards, Ren's legs gave out, and this time, he couldn't get back up.

With an arm around Ren's waist, Anik dragged him sideways towards a fallen tree. There, they all dropped to the ground, panting and gasping.

Everything was spinning. Ren felt his abdomen clench involuntarily and he bent forward and retched. Coughing, he straightened back up, the motion making stars dance before his eyes. Anik's firm hand at the back of his neck forced his head down again. Slowly, his vision returned to normal.

It felt like several minutes passed before Ren could speak. "What happened?"

"Lowlanders are mad fucks, that's what," Niklas spat.

Anik let go of Ren's neck and shot Niklas a look before answering. "They think one of us poisoned their leader."

Ren frowned, wetting his dry lips. "But I got poisoned, too."

"They don't care. Leine was going to gut you both alive. I barely managed to talk her out of it."

"Yes, what a hero you are. They still tried to shoot us down," Niklas hissed.

Ren wanted to tell them to stop arguing, but the effort of stumbling at full speed through the woods finally caught up to him. He felt himself slipping against the tree trunk, Anik's hands catching him before his head hit the ground.

When Ren woke again, it was getting dark. The first thing he noticed was that he actually felt human again. A human trampled by a dozen horses perhaps, but at least it no longer felt like the poison was boiling all his organs. The pain in his muscles was gone, except where he had gotten hurt in his fall from the horse. The nausea was gone too, although the dizziness still made him feel like he was lying on the deck of a ship.

His arms trembled slightly as he pushed himself upright. He could hear voices. Hard, angry voices. Rubbing his eyes, he looked in the direction of the sound, fearing for a moment that the refugees had found them. The forest was dark, only thin columns of fading daylight reaching down through the leaves.

"Why should I believe you? You're a thieving, murderous Lowlander. You're one of them, and you have no reason to keep Ren alive." It was Niklas' voice.

Ren focused on his friend's figure in the darkness. The moonlight reflected the steel of a dagger and Ren gasped, pushing himself onto his feet and ignoring the way his legs trembled.

"That won't end well for you," Anik said. He stood, posture relaxed, in front of Niklas with one hand outstretched towards the dagger.

"Are you threatening me?" Niklas' voice was laced with venom.

"Stop it," Ren hissed, bracing his shoulder against the trunk of a large pine tree. Niklas whipped around to face him. Anik turned more slowly and dropped his hand, although his eyes were still on the dagger.

"Both of you, that's enough," Ren said. "Niklas, put the knife away."

"How are you feeling?" Niklas' voice trembled as he sheathed the dagger and crossed the distance between them, placing a gentle hand against Ren's forehead as if to check his temperature.

"I feel better. Really," Ren assured him when he looked doubtful. Wrapping his fingers around Niklas' wrist, he dragged their hands down. Niklas turned his hand in Ren's grip to clasp it in his own.

"We're resting here for the night," Anik said, walking past them and kneeling by their bags to find something they could eat. "I think we're far enough from Sifa's camp to be safe."

"How long was I out?" Ren asked. Letting go of Niklas, he sat down on the fallen tree trunk. The daylight was fading fast.

Niklas sat down next to him. "Only a day. You were poisoned last night and you stayed unconscious until this morning," he explained. "I didn't think you'd bounce back this quickly. That Lowlander woman wasn't doing as well as you by the time we escaped."

"We should keep moving. We already wasted a day," Ren said.

"We will. Tomorrow. You need rest," Anik said, not looking up from the glowing embers of the fire.

"I'll get some more firewood," Niklas said, getting up.

Ren wanted to protest, but he knew it was no use. The twilight was fast turning into inky darkness and he doubted even Anik could find his way in the thick of the forest at night. They'd just have to hope that whatever men Halvard had sent to take Stag's Run wouldn't catch up to them in the meantime. The fort couldn't be more than a day's ride away by now.

Standing, Ren steadied himself and crossed to sit by the fire opposite Anik. One of them, probably Niklas, had dressed Ren in his new winter coat while he had been unconscious, but the cold had still managed to creep under the layers of fabric. He held out his hands, the warmth of the embers easing the stiffness out of his fingers.

Around them, pine trees stretched their needle-covered branches like eerie fingers. Pines were the only trees hardy enough to survive in the constant cold of the north, and their appearance was dark and uninviting, nothing like the oak and birch forests that surrounded Ren's home. Even in daylight, no summer birds would sing here.

Ren looked at Anik. He sat tense, hands clasped around his elbows, curled in on himself as if to soak up as much warmth from the dying fire as he could. His coat was tugged tight around his shoulders, face half hidden in the fur that lined the collar.

Around them, the ground was covered in a faint layer of frost, and their breath formed little clouds of mist in the light of the fire. Anik had probably never been somewhere this cold before. The weather in the south where the Lowlands lay was much milder. Despite the still-hot embers and the warm coat, Ren could see him shivering. Squinting, he noticed something else. A narrow gap at the front of Anik's coat revealed a dark red stain on the collar of his white undershirt.

"You're bleeding," Ren said, voice loud in the silence.

"It's not mine," Anik said softly, eyes downcast.

"You fought the refugees."

"I had to."

They both fell silent. Ren couldn't read Anik's face.

Ren watched as Anik raised his hand, fingertips grazing the dip of his throat. With a sigh, he shrugged the coat off his shoulders, tugged on the strings of his shirt, and pulled it over his head. He trembled visibly in the cold, his bare torso exposed to the chilly breeze.

"It's cold here," Anik complained, sorting through his bag to find the woollen shirt Ren had bought for him in Isleya. The fabric was thicker, better suited to the cold.

"It's the North," Ren said gently, a slight smile tugging on the corners of his lips. His eyes lingered on the scar on Anik's shoulder. It seemed to stand out even more clearly in this lighting. Ren's view was obscured when Anik pulled the clean shirt over his head and wrapped the coat back around himself, tugging the arms of his shirt through the sleeves.

159

"What happened to your shoulder?"

Anik averted his gaze, rolling his jaw. "Halvard."

Ren waited for him to say more, but he didn't. Shrugging, he continued. "What about the necklace?"

Anik's head came up, his eyes narrowing slightly as they bored into Ren's, gleaming liquid gold in the glow of the embers. A strange emotion flitted over his face. "What do you mean?"

"You keep reaching for something that isn't there," Ren explained, raising his hand to the dip of his own throat to copy the gesture.

Anik's brow creased slightly as he held Ren's gaze, and Ren waited for him to snap at him or declare that it was none of his business. Anik did neither. "It was a horseshoe," he said. "My mother gave it to me."

This time, it was Ren's turn to stare. This was unlike Anik. He never gave anything away about himself. Ren felt his curiosity grow. It was a ridiculous thing to be excited about, but Anik's walls of privacy were so high and impenetrable that even this slight glimpse into what was beyond them made Ren itch for more. Now that Anik was actually answering his questions with something other than death glares, he wanted as much as he could get before that tiny crack snapped closed once more. "Where is she?"

"She's dead," Anik said, his expression unchanging. "My whole family is." Reaching out, he carefully pushed the remaining embers closer together with a stick, then dropped the stick on top. After a moment, tiny flames licked at the wood.

"I'm sorry," Ren said. "I know how that feels."

Reaching for his pocket under the coat, Ren feared for a moment that he had lost the silver filigree key, but it was still there, nestled safely against his thigh. He closed his hand around it. *'For when you need to escape.'* His mother's last gift to him. She had seemed so healthy and strong when she had kissed his hair and stroked his back, but only a few days after giving birth to Thais, she had died in her sleep. The physician had told them it simply happened, sometimes. It made Ren glad to not have been born a woman. They risked so much bringing life to the world. His mother had carried and given birth to three children while still ruling her country. Ren had never seen her weak or faltering.

"Sifa and her people are right," Anik said, pulling Ren from his thoughts. "Skarlan is a place of horrors for our people."

Ren kept quiet, waiting for him to continue on his own. He wasn't sure why Anik was suddenly so willing to talk, but he definitely wasn't going to stop him.

"It was our land long before it was theirs. They have more soldiers and more weapons, so they can do and take whatever they want."

"We've always been told that Lowlanders attack patrols and travellers unprovoked, killing and stealing." Ren posed it almost as a question, voice gentle to avoid igniting the anger that always

161

seemed so close to the surface in Anik.

"If you had watched hundreds of people, friends and family, burn alive in their own homes and carried their scorched corpses into the woods to rest, you'd want to kill the people who'd done it, too," Anik said. His voice remained calm, but his eyes were hard as he stared at the embers as if they were to blame for all of it.

Ren wrapped his arms around himself. "But why would they do that?"

Looking up, Anik met his eyes, and Ren saw that it wasn't so much anger as frustration that shone in them. "You really have to ask? You've said exactly the same thing the soldiers always say. Lowlanders are dangerous, disgusting, vermin. We're only good dead or as slaves, right? Half the slaves in your golden city are from the Lowlands, working themselves to death in the mills and waste grounds so you can have the comfort you think you deserve. You just never see them. To you and everyone else, we're just a resource."

Ren felt himself flush in the face of the accusations. A part of him wanted to bristle, to defend his honour and the honour of his people. The pain in Anik's voice held him back. Surely not everything Anik believed was true, but maybe not everything Ren had believed was true, either. He could only imagine the agony of a hot brand against his bare neck.

"What did Halvard do to you?" he asked quietly.

162

A new kind of darkness fell over Anik's features and he wrapped his arms more tightly around himself. "He's a lot more dangerous than I think you realise."

Ren thought about their first meeting, Anik brought into Aleria in chains by the king and his advisor, Nathair as part of a plot to kill the Fraynean royal family. Ren didn't know what was so special about Anik for them to choose him for such a scheme, one Ren could still barely make sense of, as if important pieces were missing. Maybe it had just been chance. Whatever they had done to Anik, it had been bad enough for him to want revenge above everything else, so much so that he would follow Ren halfway across Frayne and injure his own countrymen for the chance that a queen's brother might give Halvard what he deserved.

A chilling howl broke the silence, deep and drawn out. The single wolf was soon joined by another.

From out of the darkness, Niklas returned with an armful of sticks. "Did you hear that?" he asked, eyes wide as he dropped the sticks next to the fire.

"Wolves don't attack people unless they're desperate, and we're a group. We'll be fine," Anik said, grabbing sticks from the pile and adding them to the fire. After a few seconds, more flames burst to life.

Despite the spreading warmth of the flames, Ren tugged his coat tighter around himself. Anik was right, the night really was quite cold, and it'd only be getting colder. It was strange to think that further south, summer was only just ending.

"The wolves aren't the only thing we should worry about," Niklas insisted, sitting down next to Ren and holding his hands out to warm them. "I've heard stories about these woods. Supposedly, groups of former slaves sought refuge here during the ice winter five years ago and went mad and started eating each other and the travellers they came across once they ran out of food. Lord Elgrin told me at the Harvest Fest last fall that he and his men found human skulls in the undergrowth when they went hunting here last summer."

"Lord Elgrin does like to make up stories," Ren said. "Remember when he tried to make everyone believe that the wine he served at his court was actually sweetened human blood?"

"It sounds like bullshit," Anik said. He was heating water over the fire in a small metal tin, carefully balancing it on a flat stone to let the flames lick at its sides.

Niklas shot Anik a glare but didn't seem in the mood to argue.

"Either way," Ren said. "We should keep watch throughout the night. We don't know how far behind us Halvard's men are or whether Sifa's refugees are still searching for us."

"Anik and I will keep watch. You need your rest," Niklas said.

Ren sighed. He wasn't sure he was completely comfortable leaving the two of them together unsupervised. Niklas had drawn a blade on Anik twice now, and Ren wasn't sure Anik would tolerate a third. Still, Niklas was right. The poison had greedily eaten away Ren's strength. He felt like he could fall asleep now and hibernate for a month.

"Wait," Anik said, holding out the tin to Ren. "Drink this."

Taking the tin from Anik, careful not to burn himself, Ren looked into it. The liquid had a yellow-green hue from the leaves Anik had added to the hot water. The smell was sharp. "What is it?"

"It's good for you. You'll need your strength back fast, especially if we have to run from people trying to kill us again."

Ren raised the tin to his lips but Niklas reached out and clasped a hand around his wrist, tugging the tin from Ren's fingers. "No, don't drink it. You don't know what's in it."

"You really think I'd poison him when I could just stab my sword through his gut and be done with it?" Anik asked dryly as Niklas demonstratively emptied the contents of the tin onto the ground.

"For all I know, you already tried to poison him once. Maybe you're so twisted that you want to see him die a slow death," Niklas hissed.

Ren sighed and rubbed his brow with two fingers. "Niklas, calm down. Please try not to kill each other while I sleep. I mean it," Ren said, letting his gaze linger on both of them before he got up from the fallen log to fetch his blankets.

165

Ren felt like he had only been asleep for a few hours before he was shaken awake. Groaning, he sat up, blinking sleep from his eyes.

"There's a wagon approaching." Niklas was kneeling in front of him. It was completely dark, only faint embers remaining in the fire, which had been stomped out rather than burned out, judging by the dirt tracks that surrounded it.

Next to them, Anik tossed his blankets aside and sat up straight. He looked wide awake.

Dancing torchlight was the first thing Ren saw as the wagon approached. At first, it seemed to come straight for them, but then the dirt path curved around their makeshift camp. This close, Ren could see that the wagon was pulled by two horses, driven by one man, and carrying passengers.

Ren glanced at Anik, trying to figure out what his course of action would be. When Anik stood, reaching for his sword, Ren did the same. He doubted he could fight anyone in his current condition, but sometimes the threat of multiple swords was enough to deter attackers. Niklas kept close to Ren, watching him carefully like he was afraid he was going to collapse.

"Who goes there?" Anik called out. He held his sword casually at his side, slowly stepping towards the narrow trail. Ren heard a soft command from the wagon driver as he slowed the horses. Ren stayed where he was.

"This is a bad idea," Niklas whispered. "We should have stayed hidden. He's trying to get us killed."

Ren hushed him.

Stopping beside the wagon, Anik tilted his head back and spoke to the driver too quietly for Ren to hear. After a short exchange of words, Anik turned around and sheathed his sword.

"They're going our way. We can hitch a ride," Anik said when he reached them.

"No way." Niklas shook his head vehemently.

Anik raised an eyebrow and turned to Ren. "Do you want to walk for half a day through the woods in your condition?"

Ren hesitated. So far, Anik hadn't been wrong about anything.

"We don't know who they are. They could be murderers," Niklas argued, voice tense.

"Right. Murderers travelling through the woods with a kid and four bags of grain," Anik replied, rolling his eyes.

"Let's do it," Ren decided. "Anik is right. Berin said Skarlan soldiers are riding for Stag's Run. We won't make it in time if we're on foot."

Niklas opened his mouth to argue, but Ren was already grabbing their bags and passing one to Anik. Anik took the strap of the other bag as well and Ren let go without protest. His muscles felt like pudding.

However ominous a ride in a strange wagon in the middle of the night seemed, it was a risk they had to take. Nothing was more important than getting to Stag's Run. They had to help Lord Tyke reclaim the throne. They had to get Thais away from King Halvard.

The wagon driver nodded in greeting as they approached and Ren worried for a moment that he would ask for some kind of compensation they wouldn't be able to provide, but the man stayed silent. Anik hopped onto the wagon and reached down to help Ren up. Ren didn't miss the glare Niklas sent the Lowlander or the way he hurried to seat himself next to Anik on the bench so Ren had to take the end seat. Hopefully once they reached Stag's Run, Niklas and Anik could get out of each other's way.

On opposite sides of the wagon on the end closest to the driver sat two men. The one next to Anik was hidden from Ren's view, but the other was maybe thirty and had fiery ginger hair. In front of Ren sat a young women and a boy of maybe ten. Ren offered the woman a smile and gave the boy a wave. He waved back. Anik had been right; these people didn't look anything like murderers.

"You a Lowlander?" the ginger-haired man asked, leaning towards Anik. His accent was similar to Anik's and Ren found himself wondering just how many Lowlanders there were in Frayne. The children in Isleya, Ilias, the refugees, these travellers. More than he had known, evidently.

Anik answered in their own language and Ren tuned out the soft sound of their voices.

The night was cold and the road was bumpy, but Ren was thankful to not have to travel all the way on foot. His bones and muscles still ached. Any thoughts of food sent his stomach into a twist.

He had really been poisoned. He could have died. The more he thought about it, the more that reality seemed to strike home. He had survived an attempt on his life by some unknown attacker. It could have been anyone.

The poison had been in the second keg. Only he and Sifa had drunk from it. There was a possibility that the contents of the keg had already been poisoned by the time the refugees stole it, but he couldn't think of any reason Skarlans would poison alcohol they were drinking themselves. Ren looked across at Anik. Niklas was still convinced that Anik had been the one to do it, but Anik had a point: if he'd wanted Ren dead, he could have put a sword through his gut at any time. Ren had conveniently supplied him with a weapon with which to do so. Then again, Ren clearly remembered Anik refusing the bowl of kalg poured from the second keg that Sifa had offered him. As if he had known.

Somewhere in the distance, a wolf howled again. The sound of the horses' hooves was muffled by the soft forest soil. Other than that, the night was silent.

"What's your name?"

Niklas' voice pulled Ren from his thoughts and he looked across at the young boy swaying in his seat, clearly tired but refusing to succumb to sleep.

"I'm Lyle. This is my sister Ira," the boy said, gesturing to the young woman next to him before suppressing a yawn. He spoke in a slight country dialect. The bridge of his nose was dusted with dark freckles of the kind that seemed permanently prominent, regardless of the season. The freckles that covered Ren's own nose and cheeks were fainter and faded in the winter.

"What are you doing up here?" Ren asked, leaning his arms against the edge of the wagon.

It was Ira who answered. "Our family owns a farm two days' ride from here. Once a month, we take fresh supplies up to Stag's Run," she said, angling her chin at the bags of grain. "Our father is stationed there."

"Isn't it a bad idea to travel through the woods in the middle of the night?" Niklas asked.

Ira nodded. "It's not something we normally do, but our timing was a bit off this time. By the time the sun went down, we had already reached the edge of the forest and we thought it'd be best not to camp here. Being on the move is safer. You three are either very brave or very stupid to have tried staying the night," she said, offering Ren and Niklas a small smile.

"See? I told you there was good reason to be on guard," Niklas murmured.

"We didn't really have much of an option," Ren said. He glanced to the side at the two men, both of them now engaged in conversation with Anik. "And those two?"

"Hmm?" Ira followed his eyes. "Oh, they're travellers, I think. They wanted to hitch a ride, just like you three."

"They're Lowlanders."

Ira shrugged. "Yes, but they seem nice enough. They even wanted to pay, but we never take payment for extra passengers."

"What are Lowlanders doing this far north, though?" Niklas asked. "There are no more villages beyond the forest."

"Looking for work, I suppose. Stag's Run is always looking for extra hands," Ira said.

"Look," Lyle said, drawing a small dagger from a sheath in his belt. It had a simple, leather wrapped hilt and a single edge. "My father gave me this."

"That's a mighty fine sword," Niklas said, making the boy giggle.

Turning slightly, Ren rested his side against the corner of the wagon. A cloud passed in front of the moon, casting the forest into darkness made even more apparent by the light of the torches.

Closing his eyes, he thought about Hellic, how proud he had looked in his brand new armour with the engraved antlers curling upwards on the breastplate, how happy he had been the morning of his birthday at the prospect of a thrilling boar hunt. The kill had been Ren's for the taking, but he had wanted Hellic to have it, just to see the joy on his face. He would have done anything for his brother. Hellic was supposed to be the king Frayne deserved.

Ren smiled to himself at the memory of their late lunches under the apple trees in the garden. Hellic had been so worried about his future marriage. Ren had told him he could refuse if he wanted to. But Hellic knew, because his father had told him, that marriages between powerful families were assets to a kingdom, and Hellic wanted nothing more than to do what was best for Frayne. They had laughed so much that day, eating apples right off the tree. Hellic had teased Ren about the young Lady Arrika with the chestnut curls that Ren had been eyeing all summer.

"There's nothing between us. It was just a flirt," Ren had assured him. "She's leaving for the Eastern Islands in a few days, after all."

"Well," Hellic had replied, a mischievous glint in his eye. "You can always go back to fucking that servant boy with the big brown eyes you like to drown your sorrows in."

Ren had pushed Hellic off his seat and onto his back on the grass and they had both laughed again. Hellic had been right. When Lady Arrika left, it was exactly what Ren had done.

Suddenly, complete darkness fell. Ren opened his eyes, but it was just as dark as it had been behind his eyelids. The torches had gone out. Eyes wide in the darkness, Ren heard the driver stop the horses with a soft sound, the wagon rolling to a halt.

"Just a moment," the driver said. Then came the sounds of what Ren assumed was the driver searching for fresh torches in the darkness.

Ren sat up straight. Lyle whimpered quietly.

"It'll be all right," Ren said. "Stag's Run isn't far, now."

Ren held his hands up in front of his face. It really was pitch black, the thick clouds blocking what little moonlight might have made it through the trees.

Ren felt movement to his left, a nudge of his shoulder. "Niklas?"

There was a dull sliding sound Ren couldn't quite place, followed by a sound much worse: ripping, a choked-out gasp, the sound a person makes when blood floods their lungs. Someone fell to the floor of the wagon and Lyle cried out in fear.

"Where's the light?" Ren called, reaching for his sword with his heart in his throat. Something was very wrong, and Ren felt like a blind fly in a spider's web. "Where's the damn light?"

CHAPTER EIGHT

Commotion.

A startled shout. It sounded like Anik, but Ren couldn't be sure.

The sharp pain of a blade slicing through the skin of his upper arm made Ren stagger to his feet. He backed up and stepped right into thin air.

With a cry, he landed on his back in the forest leaf litter.

"Niklas!" he called. He hadn't let go of his sword in the fall and he gripped it even tighter as he pushed himself to his feet, stars dancing in front of his eyes. The aftereffects of the poison left him panting, out of breath, although maybe it was fear making his heart race.

Raising his sword, Ren took a few steps backwards, feeling

dead leaves and branches shift under his boots. When he held back a hand, he felt the rough bark of a tree against his palm. Warm blood trickled down his arm, making his sleeve stick to his skin.

Slowly, the clouds drifted away from the moon and gilded the forest scene in a faint, ghostly light. Ren saw figures moving in the dark: someone running, two people struggling. It was impossible to make out who was who. "Anik!"

A hard body slammed into Ren's side and he tumbled onto the ground, gasping for air. The world spun. He had dropped his sword. Head spinning, Ren shuffled backward in an attempt to find his weapon, grasping handfuls of leaves and dirt.

The man with whom he had collided rolled on top of Ren, straddling his hips and bearing down on him with his weight. It was one of the Lowlanders, the man who had sat on Anik's other side, hidden from Ren's view. He was large and strong, pinning Ren effortlessly as he reached back and drew a dagger from his belt.

Gasping, Ren raised his hands and gripped the man's wrist just in time to stop the blade from slicing into his throat. Frantically, he looked around. Where was his sword?

The man raised his other hand, fingers curling into a fist. Unable to defend himself, all Ren could do was turn his head away and clench his eyes shut. The punch rattled his jaw and he groaned, kicking his legs in an attempt to free himself. Letting go of the man's wrist with one hand, he reached back, trying to find something, anything, he could use to defend himself.

His fingers curled around a cold, jagged stone.

Gripping it tightly, he put all his strength into the strike and slammed the stone against his attacker's temple. The man went limp, falling half on top of Ren. Shoving him away, Ren scrambled back to his feet, staggering before he caught his balance with a hand against the trunk of a tree.

Ren stared at the man. His eyes were open, but his body was still. He was dead. Ren had killed him; he had really killed a man. Light-headedness threatened to make him topple over, and it wasn't just the effects of the poison this time. He couldn't take his eyes off the corpse.

A sudden light made Ren squint and he looked up to see that the torches were lit. The driver, still seated on the wagon, had drawn a knife, eyes wide with fear, but the fight seemed to have avoided him.

Ren glanced back at the dead man. His hair was ginger, like the man Anik had been talking to. His brother, then. That was who had been sitting on Anik's other side. The two Lowlanders had been brothers. A fresh wave of nausea overcame him and he squeezed his eyes shut.

"Ren!" Niklas' voice broke through the silence and Ren whirled around, finally tearing his gaze from the body.

"Are you all right?" Ren asked, voice sounding hollow in his own ears. "What happened?"

Niklas was pale in the light of the flames. Anik's sword was in his hand. There was blood on the blade.

"I don't know," Niklas replied, looking shaken. His hand trembled when he ran it through his hair. "When the lights went out, someone shoved me. Then Anik attacked me. I managed to pry his sword from him in the darkness and knock him out. I…I think he was going to kill me, Ren."

"Wait," Ren said, a chill rushing through his body that had nothing to do with the cold. "Anik?"

"I told you he was dangerous. You've seen how strange he's been acting."

Looking over Niklas' shoulder, Ren spotted Anik on the ground. His eyes were closed and a line of blood ran from his forehead and along his temple.

"And the blood?" Ren asked, gesturing to the sword in Niklas' hand.

"I don't know," Niklas replied. "I think Anik stabbed that Lowlander on the wagon."

Ren frowned, struggling to make sense of it all. "But he's a Lowlander himself. Why would he kill his own people? They were just talking."

Niklas shook his head. "Fuck if I know. You saw the way he fought those refugees. He poisoned the drink. Lowlanders are soulless, Ren. We've known that all along. If he did this to his own people..."

Ren looked back at the man he had killed. The man had attacked, enraged, trying to protect or avenge the brother Anik had killed. Ren had just been the closest target.

He turned his gaze on Anik. He had seemed like an honourable man. Pessimistic, rough, and rude, perhaps, but Ren had at least trusted that he was a reasonable person. The poison, this blind attack...they made no sense at all. Maybe Niklas was right – maybe it was impossible to expect decency or even logical behaviour from Lowlanders. If so, Anik didn't care who got hurt or how, simply that they did. Maybe Halvard had twisted him into that kind of person during his time as the king's slave.

"Ren? What should we do?"

"All right," Ren said finally. "Let's tie him up and put him on the wagon."

"Why can't we just leave him?"

"I need to know what's really going on. We'll put him in a cell when we reach Stag's Run."

Locating his sword, Ren sheathed it. The driver watched them with caution as they approached the wagon, but he apparently put two and two together at the sight of the dead Lowlanders. Ren asked for lengths of rope and the driver untied some from around the bags of grain. Ren passed them to Niklas.

"Will you still drive us?" Ren asked.

The driver nodded, lips pressed tight.

Ren looked around. Lyle and Ira were nowhere to be seen. Unease crept up Ren's spine, but then a faint sound made him crouch down and look under the wagon. Ira flinched at the sight of him, clutching his brother tighter against her chest.

"It's all right. You're safe now," Ren assured them, voice soft as he extended a hand. He helped the two of them to their feet and Ira covered Lyle's eyes as the driver dragged the body of the dead Lowlander off the wagon.

"They seemed like nice people. I had no idea... We wouldn't have..." Ira's voice shook.

"It wasn't your fault," Ren said. Placing a hand on her shoulder, he gave it a squeeze. "Lowlanders are sly and deceptive." He glanced to where Niklas was tying Anik's wrists together.

"You'd do well not to trust their kind again," Niklas said over his shoulder. "Ren, help me lift him."

Ren grabbed Lyle by the hips and helped him up onto the wagon, then returned to Niklas. "I owe you an apology," he said quietly. Above them, the sky was lightening with the first hints of morning light. "I should have listened to you."

Niklas shook his head. "Don't apologize. I'm just glad you're alive."

Together, they carried Anik's limp body to the wagon. Lyle eyed the bound Lowlander nervously and inched closer to his sister.

It had been stupid of Ren to trust Anik. Maybe he had just been desperate to have someone on his side, someone to watch his back in a world where suddenly everyone seemed to be the enemy. But he had Niklas, now. He didn't need the Lowlander ex-slave. Ren's whole body ached and his head pounded when he climbed into the wagon and let Niklas wrap an arm around his shoulders.

* * *

Stag's Run came into view beyond the cliffs a few hours after dawn. Situated at the mouth of the narrow passage that led to the vast North, the stronghold protected one of Frayne's greatest resources. It was a magnificent sight, with mountaintops that reached into the clouds, casting the fort nestled between them in shadow. The building itself looked small in comparison, but it was an illusion. Stag's Run was an impressive fort with curving battlements, two watchtowers, and barracks large enough to house a thousand soldiers. A wide moat spanned the entire front of the fort, chiselled into the stony ground from one side of the passage to the other.

Pure relief flooded Ren as they approached. This was it. Lord Tyke would claim the throne of Aleria. Thais would be released. They could keep this disaster from getting any worse and Ren could return home. Halvard would get the punishment he deserved, and if that meant another war with Skarlan, then so be it. Frayne was strong, and its people wouldn't accept invasion lying down. Stag's Run was a prime example of that.

The wagon came to a stop in front of the moat. Ren looked up at the towers. No one called out at their arrival. It was dead silent.

"Hey," the driver called out. "Grain delivery."

A long moment passed before something happened. A man appeared in the tower, waved at them, and signalled for the gate to be opened.

Slowly, the little wagon rolled over the stone bridge and into the courtyard.

Ren stared. He had expected it to be buzzing with activity, but the courtyard was as empty as the towers had been. A feeling of abandonment lay heavy over the place, which seemed quiet and worn.

Frowning, Ren looked across at Ira and Lyle, but they didn't seem fazed. "Is it always like this?"

Meeting his eyes, Ira nodded. "It has been for a while, now."

Ren glanced at Niklas, who shrugged, looking just as confused as Ren felt.

At last, a small group of people approached them from the large double doors of the fort: a man Ren could only assume was the fort commander, and two soldiers, a man and a woman. One of the soldiers, the man, smiled widely.

"Father!" Lyle leapt off the wagon and straight into the

smiling soldier's arms. Ira followed at a steadier pace and the man straightened up to kiss her brow and include her in his embrace.

Ren averted his gaze, a familiar ache building in his chest. He turned his attention to the commander, who greeted the wagon driver like an old friend. "Sir. My name is Ren Frayne, son of her late Majesty the Queen," he announced. "I've come because I require the aid of my uncle, Lord Tyke." Reaching for his sword, he unsheathed it halfway to display the golden stag symbol engraved in the crossguard. After living like a common traveller for close to a week, it was a rush to introduce himself with his proper title.

The reaction was immediate.

The commander turned towards Ren, lips slowly parting before he regained his composure and dropped to one knee. Instantly, the two soldiers followed his example, although Ira and Lyle's father kept hold of his childrens' hands. After a moment, Ira kneeled as well. Lyle shuffled his feet, staring openly at Ren with wide eyes.

"My lord," the commander said, eyes trained on the ground. "We welcome you to Stag's Run. We're honoured to have you and we'll aid you in any way we can. I'll inform Lord Tyke of your arrival at once."

Ren let out a breath of relief. A small part of him had been worried that the false words of his crime had already made it to

Stag's Run. "Thank you. On your feet, Commander," Ren said, climbing off the wagon, followed by Niklas. He pointed to Anik. Anik's eyes were closed and he hadn't moved at all during their journey to the fort. Ren didn't know if he was still unconscious or if he was simply pretending. "Place the prisoner in a cell."

"And get a physician. The prince is injured," Niklas added, nodding to the cut on Ren's arm.

Ren looked down. The cut was shallow and the blood had dried hours ago. "It can wait," he said. "I'll see my uncle first."

The commander directed Ren to Lord Tyke's private chambers, not the audience hall. Inside, the fort was as silent as the courtyard. A guard informed him that they had turned the audience hall into a storage room years ago, since people only rarely visited the northern front. That should have been Ren's first hint.

Lord Tyke was nothing like Ren remembered him.

As he stepped into the lord's chambers, Ren's boot bumped an empty bottle, which rolled across the floor. The room was a mess. Clothes and armour were tossed on the floor, papers strewn on the table, the bed unmade. The room clearly hadn't seen servants in a long time.

Lord Tyke sat in an armchair by the desk. He looked up from his book as Ren entered, surprise flitting over his features. "Is that really you? My sister's bastard? No one sent word that you'd be joining us." He waved Ren closer.

183

"Hello, Uncle."

Judging by Lord Tyke's physique, it had been a while since he'd last had to fight in the defence of Stag's Run. He had grown soft. The taut muscles Ren remembered from his childhood were long gone, and his chin was covered in chicken grease that he apparently hadn't bothered to wipe off his face after his breakfast.

None of that mattered, Ren told himself. The capabilities of a king didn't rely on the appearance of his body or his chambers.

"I'm assuming you haven't gotten word from Aleria," Ren said, taking a seat at the desk opposite his uncle, who poured him a cup of wine. Ren took a sip, then clasped his hands under the table, trying his best to ignore the nervousness that crept under his skin.

"Go on," Lord Tyke said.

There was no easy way to say it. Ren stole a steadying breath. "The king and my brother, the crown prince, are dead."

Lord Tyke's expression froze, then warped into disbelief, followed by shock. "What are you saying, boy?" he spluttered, and almost knocked over his wine cup.

"They were assassinated a week ago, on my brother's birthday, by the king of Skarlan, who was in attendance."

Relief filled Ren, relief at finally being able to tell these things to someone who could help, who could take the crushing responsibility off his shoulders. He wasn't a general, or a leader, or a king in the making. He was just a fortunate boy born into royalty.

"The king of Skarlan." Lord Tyke spoke slowly, gripping his wine cup until his knuckles turned white. Ren saw his chest expand before he raised the cup to his lips and drained the contents, then refilled it to the brim.

"He currently holds the throne of Frayne with Prince Thais as his hostage."

"What does he want?" Lord Tyke asked, rubbing a hand over his mouth.

"He wants to marry Thais to his daughter and claim Frayne as part of his kingdom," Ren explained. "Frayne and Skarlan are the two greatest nations in this part of the world. If he sits on both thrones, he can wage wars across the sea. He'll be nearly unstoppable."

"He doesn't have the resources," Lord Tyke said, shaking his head as he leaned back in his chair.

"But he will," Ren insisted. "He's sending soldiers to Stag's Run as we speak. He'll take possession of the North. With the resources there, he can build weapons and ships. From there, it'll be no problem for him to take the southern trade routes as well. He will-"

"Hold on, boy," Lord Tyke said, stopping Ren with a hand in the air before taking another gulp of his wine, hand shaking. "Why are you here? Why did you come all this way to tell me this?"

185

Ren swallowed hard, fists clenched against his thighs. "You must ride back to Aleria with me. You're the queen's brother; you have the right to the title as regent until Prince Thais comes of age. You can stop the marriage and kick Halvard out of our country," Ren said, tension in his voice as he leaned forward. "It's our only chance."

"You want me to rule," Lord Tyke said flatly, sounding as though Ren had just asked him to eat cow dung.

"For a few years. Yes."

"Absolutely not."

"But-"

"You're out of your mind, boy. If the king and the crown prince are dead, then it's out of our hands." Lord Tyke stood up, chair scraping against the floor as he walked over to the window.

Ren's breath caught in his throat. He hadn't considered that Tyke might refuse. It had simply never occurred to him. The safety of the nation came above all else, that and the safety of everyone he knew and cared about back home who currently had the blades of Skarlan swords pressed to their throats.

Getting up, Ren followed Tyke to the window. "My mother would want-"

"Your mother is dead," Lord Tyke said, and the force of his words made Ren take half a step back. When he turned back to look at Ren, his face was bright red. "After your mother died, King Callun stopped giving a shit about me. Left me to rot in this rat hole. Look at it," he hissed, gesturing to the window. "Stag's Run is falling apart. This is the kind of place people go to retire, and that's exactly what I plan on doing." Grabbing the bottle of wine, he inverted it and took several gulps before setting it down on the table, hard. "I want nothing to do with my sister's kingdom. I intend to stay here, be left alone, and eat myself fat on chicken and beef. And if you for one second think that a bastard boy like you can somehow save this nation, then you're as naïve and gullible as my sister was."

Ren's entire body went tense, nails digging into his palms. No, he had not come all this way for... Failure was not an option. "I don't think you understand what this means. We-"

"Let it go!" Lord Tyke's voice boomed, too loud for the cluttered chamber, but when he spoke again, it was quietly. "Your mother fought for the wrong reasons, and now she's dead. If King Halvard sits on the Fraynean throne now, then that's how it is, and all the rest of us can do is hope he'll be a merciful king. If he's searching for you, then I suggest you take a horse and get as far away from Frayne as you can. That's what I would do."

Ren narrowed his eyes, his jaw working. How could he say such a thing? How could he watch everything his family had fought so hard for shatter and do nothing to save it? The king was dead. The crown prince was dead. And all Lord Tyke cared about was wine and chicken. "I didn't know the queen's brother was such a heartless fucking coward," he said, the words coming out

187

hard and sharp.

The sound of the slap resounded in the room and Ren's head jerked to the side. For a moment, Ren stood, stunned. He tasted blood, metallic in his mouth where he had bitten his tongue. Slowly, he raised his hand to his face. Ignoring the frustrated tears welling up in his eyes, Ren opened his mouth to speak, to try again. He'd drag Lord Tyke back to Aleria if he had to.

He didn't get a chance to say anything before the door to his uncle's chambers opened. It was a man in his mid-twenties or so, dressed in the same soldier's uniform they all wore, but his right jacket sleeve had been severed and sewn together at the shoulder to better suit his missing arm. When Ren raised his gaze, he saw that the same side of his face was heavily scarred.

"Please excuse my interruption," the young man said quietly, ignoring the clutter in the room as he looked between Ren and Lord Tyke. Judging by his cautious expression, he had heard Lord Tyke's shouting. "A messenger just arrived. He's waiting in the courtyard and he says he'll only speak to the prince. He says it's urgent."

Ren spun on his heel and left the chambers without another glance at Lord Tyke. He'd have to talk to him again later, make him understand what was at stake. He let the door fall shut behind him.

"Forgive me, but Lord Tyke didn't sound pleased," the young soldier noted as he led Ren through the rough stone corridors.

188

"He wasn't." Ren glanced at the man. The scars on the side of his face did little to detract from his good looks. He was handsome, with a sharp jawline, brown eyes, and long lashes. His skin had the same golden hue as Anik's. In Aleria, Ren might have taken him to bed. Such thoughts seemed shallow and unimportant, now. "What's your name?"

"Jayce, my lord. I'm a physician. And a soldier, and a messenger." He rubbed the back of his neck with a crooked smile. "Whatever I'm needed to be. A physician first and foremost, however. If you'd like, I can tend to that cut at your leisure."

Ren nodded. "Is it true, what Lord Tyke told me? That Stag's Run is falling apart? Where are all the men?"

Jayce frowned. "It's true," he confirmed. "Stag's Run hasn't seen a real threat in many years. Certainly not in the time I've been here. Not that I mind so much, personally, my lord. I needed time to recover," he added, gesturing to his missing arm. "And with one blind eye and one deaf ear, I'm not as sharp in a fight as I used to be."

Ren glanced at Jayce, noticing now the milkiness of his right eye. His ear was torn and jagged.

Jayce continued. "The fort isn't exactly in its prime. The foundations of the western battlements are crumbling and our weapons and equipment have seen better days. We're also painfully undermanned. No one wants to stay here long when all

189

we do every day is throw spears at targets and freeze our asses off. Excuse my language."

"Understandable," Ren said, feeling some of his childhood fantasies about the place shatter.

They left the dark corridors behind and exited into the courtyard, the double doors pushed open by a pair of guards who seemed to have been stationed there only after Ren's arrival.

The messenger was still on horseback, standing at the foot of the stone stairs. The animal's coat was damp with sweat and its mouth dripped with foam. He had been riding hard.

Leaving Jayce behind by the doors, Ren took the stairs two at a time. A guard stood on either side of the messenger. Ren stopped just over a sword's length away and gestured for the man to speak.

"Are you Prince Ren of Frayne?" the messenger asked, drawing his hood back. He was a man in his forties, wavy black hair shot through with grey framing his face.

"I am," Ren said. "I understand you have urgent information. Do you wish to come inside?"

Even before Ren was done talking, the messenger shook his head. Niklas came down the steps to join Ren and the two of them exchanged a quick glance. "Who sent you?" Ren asked.

"I can't say," the messenger said, withdrawing a folded note from his breast pocket. "This is my message."

Ren stepped closer and accepted the note from the rider and

turned it over. No sigil.

The clatter of hooves against stone made him raise his head. The messenger had turned away and galloped out of the fort and across the moat. Slowly, the gate closed again.

"What was that all about?" Niklas asked, gaze lingering on the fort gate.

Ren shook his head. Crossing the courtyard with Niklas trailing behind him, he stopped in the shade of a stone pillar and leaned against the balustrade. Unfolding the note, Ren frowned.

One hundred and ten Skarlan soldiers will arrive at Stag's Run at noon tomorrow.

The note, written in black ink on parchment paper, gave away nothing of the sender besides a small symbol in the bottom right corner.

"Is that a fox?" Niklas asked, leaning over Ren's shoulder to look.

"I think so," Ren said. He swiped his thumb over the slightly raised stamp.

"Who has a fox as their sigil?"

"No one I know of," Ren said, folding the note.

"Maybe we shouldn't trust it."

"It can't hurt to be prepared," Ren argued, casting a glance out over the empty courtyard. "Go to the commander and tell him I

191

want men stationed in the towers. Say they need to report even the slightest disturbance. I want scouts in the area, too." It seemed like something King Callun would have done.

* * *

Ren leaned his elbows against the lichen-covered battlement and gazed out over the passage to the North. Only a day ago, their plan had been so clear. Stag's Run had seemed like a beacon of hope and strength. Now, it was all falling apart. Lord Tyke had rejected him, Skarlan soldiers were marching upon Stag's Run at this very moment, and the fort was nowhere near able to defend itself, with too few soldiers, not enough weapons, and a crumbling foundation. How had King Callun let it get to this state?

Ren had grown up thinking of Stag's Run as a glowing symbol of Fraynean pride, the powerful guardian of the gate to their bountiful wealth. The reality was grim by comparison. And it wasn't a recent development, either. Jayce had made that much clear when he had cleaned and bandaged Ren's arm in the dining hall.

Lord Tyke had been alerted of the approaching force, but had done nothing so far. As prince, Ren could overrule his authority and prepare the fort for siege himself, but what use would that be? He wasn't a military leader. He had never seen a war. A

Lowlander slave could beat him in a sword fight in under thirty seconds. The man he had killed in the woods had been the first time he had ever taken a life, and the thought of it still made his stomach twist.

Maybe this was the end. Maybe this entire idea of saving the kingdom had been a pipe dream. Of course it was never going to be this easy.

Quiet footsteps against the stone of the battlement made Ren turn, but he relaxed at the sight of his Niklas. His friend gave him a sad smile and came to stand next to him.

"The commander has stationed two guards in each tower at your orders," Niklas said, tugging his warm coat closer around himself against the chill wind.

"Good."

"What are you going to do now?"

"I don't know," Ren said quietly.

Ahead, the passage to the North cut through the mountains like a narrow, twisting river of stone. Fat brown cattle, the soldiers' source of fresh milk and meat, grazed on the gentle slopes at the base of the fort, seeking out the scattered patches of grass hidden under the shallow layer of snow.

"I'm so sorry about your brother, Ren. And King Callun. I know he was like a father to you."

Ren swallowed hard and nodded. He didn't speak until he was sure his voice wouldn't fail him. He closed his hand tight around the hilt of his brother's sword where it was strapped to his hip. "Hellic would know what to do."

Niklas moved closer. Warm fingers slipped around the inside of Ren's wrist and Ren allowed it. He hadn't realised until now how much he had craved such a soft, physical touch. Turning his hand, he laced their fingers together.

"Callun didn't want me at that party. What if I had just listened and it had stopped all this from happening?"

"I don't think you could have," Niklas said, squeezing his hand. "Maybe…" he continued, and seemed to search for words carefully, "Maybe the best option now is to just return to Aleria."

Ren frowned, taking his eyes off the view to look at Niklas. "He'll kill us."

"Maybe he won't," Niklas said, straightening up and looking at Ren with wide eyes. He squeezed his hand tighter. "If we try talking to him, maybe he'll listen. You're a bastard; you can't threaten his place on the throne. He might let us back in, and then you can watch over Thais."

"His place on the throne…"

"You know my heritage," Niklas continued, gripping Ren's hand in both of his own. "My father was a high-ranking general, a friend of King Halvard. He'll listen to me and I can vouch for you. Surely, he'll at least listen."

Breath catching in his throat, Ren yanked his hands free of Niklas' grasp and took a step back. "What are you saying?" he

194

asked, staring at Niklas. "You really want me to bow to the man who slaughtered my family? It was your family, too," Ren rasped.

"The Lowlander killed your family."

"And you honestly think Halvard will just let Thais grow up and then politely pass the throne to him? That's not going to happen. Halvard will slaughter him like he slaughtered Hellic," Ren said, the sharpness of his voice making the guards stationed on the battlements across the courtyard turn and stare.

"You don't know that!" Niklas said. "We can make a deal. I'm sure he'll be reasonable. Halvard came to my chambers and spoke to me before I left Aleria. He told me amazing stories about my parents, he really respected them, Ren. We can at least try, I just don't want you to die," Niklas said, his voice trembling. His eyes were red-rimmed.

Ren's heart raced. He couldn't believe this. Niklas was suggesting surrendering their entire country to the Skarlan king exactly as Lord Tyke had done. Niklas and Halvard had shared a private, friendly conversation in Niklas' chambers and Niklas had listened. Shaking his head, he spun on his heel. This was too much. He needed to get away, he needed to think, to salvage the little bits of truth he still had left. He heard Niklas calling out his name, but didn't stop. His feet carried him along the battlements, through a tower door and down a flight of stairs.

Finding himself in a dark work room, he stumbled to a halt.

Lord Tyke stood bent over a dust-covered desk, scribbling away on a piece of curling letter paper in the light of a single candle. At the sound of Ren's boots against the steps, he looked up, snatched the letter and folded it closed. "This place is private. Get out," Lord Tyke said, voice strained as he glared at Ren.

"Who are you writing to?" Ren asked, all his frustration and hopelessness focused into a bitter ball of resentment.

"It's none of your business, boy. Get out," his uncle spat, face reddening.

In an instant, Ren drew his sword. He held it steadily, point aimed at Tyke. "Show me the letter," he said, voice harder than he had known it capable.

"How dare you draw your sword on your own uncle, you rat?" Lord Tyke spluttered.

Ren stepped forward, silencing the older man by pressing the tip of his sword against his throat. Slowly, Lord Tyke brought his hand forward and held out the piece of paper, face red with anger.

Snatching it, Ren took a few steps back. He kept his sword raised as he glanced down at the hastily scribbled words.

Addressed to the approaching enemy, the letter detailed the fort's troop count and weapons, as well as descriptions of a hidden entryway into the keep on the east side. Lastly, it contained a plea for protection from King Halvard and a request to return to Aleria for retirement in exchange for the information provided.

Ren stared at the letter. Treason. Ren's gut twisted painfully. Two members of his family had betrayed him in the span of only minutes. Had the Stags really been such horrible rulers that they deserved this kind of treatment?

Distracted by the letter, Ren didn't see the attack before it was too late.

His sword was shoved aside and a hard kick to his chest knocked the air from his lungs. He staggered backward, shoulder hitting a shelf, which collapsed and sent old jars tumbling to shatter on the ground.

Lord Tyke might have grown lazy and slow in the quiet years spent in Stag's Run, but he had been a skilled warrior once, better than Ren by a long shot.

Closing the space between them in two strides, Lord Tyke closed his hand tight around Ren's wrist and twisted. Pain shot through his arm and Ren gritted his teeth, forced to release the sword, which fell to the ground with a clatter. He tried to shove and kick, but Lord Tyke pinned him against the wall with the entire weight of his body. The lingering effects of the poison remained, draining the strength from Ren's muscles fast.

"I don't want to hurt you. Stop resisting," Lord Tyke growled, his weight against Ren's chest making it hard to breathe.

Opening his mouth to shout, Ren felt Tyke's large hand clamp tight around his throat. Ren tried to twist away, but Tyke's grip on him was like a vice. His lungs burned with the need for air, sparks dancing at the edges of his vision. He wasn't strong enough. He couldn't win this fight.

CHAPTER NINE

So this was how he would die. Not shot down in an open field or poisoned by strangers, not even cut down in his attempt to defend Frayne's most important fort. No, he would be choked to death by his uncle in a crumbling tower where his body likely wouldn't be found for several hours, not until someone started to wonder where the young bastard boy might have gone. Dead, only a few months after his twenty-second summer.

Darkness ate its way across his vision as his entire body screamed for air. He clawed at Tyke's wrists, but it was no use.

Somewhere far away, a door slammed back on its hinges, the slam followed by the sound of shouting men.

In the next moment, the pressure against Ren's throat

disappeared and a rush of air filled his lungs. Head spinning, he staggered to the side and caught himself against the table as his surroundings slowly came back into view.

Jayce was in the room with them. He had drawn a long, sleek dagger and held it pressed to Lord Tyke's throat, backing him against the wall. Ren wanted to warn him of Tyke's strength, but when he parted his lips, he could only cough.

"Men!" Jayce shouted over his shoulder, glancing briefly at Ren as if to make sure he was still on his feet. Several soldiers rushed into the room, gripped Tyke by the elbows and twisted his arms behind his back.

"Release me! This is treason. I will have all your heads on stakes, you worthless dogs!" Lord Tyke hissed and spluttered, forcing Jayce to take several steps back to avoid a spray of spittle.

Ren coughed again, his throat tender as he drew a breath. When he spoke, his voice was barely louder than a whisper before it regained some of its strength. "He was writing to the enemy." Bending down to pick up the letter he had dropped, he handed it to Jayce with faintly trembling fingers. "Throw him in a cell."

The soldiers dragged the furious lord out of the room. Ren could hear his curses and insults all across the courtyard until Jayce closed the door.

Ren sank down into the chair by the desk, running a hand over his sore throat.

"Are you all right?" Jayce asked, tearing the letter into pieces and letting them float to the floor. He came forward and leaned against the table next to Ren, placing his hand on Ren's shoulder.

Ren nodded, closing his eyes for a long moment. "I just wasn't expecting things to get worse than they already were."

"I don't know if this is worse," Jayce said, offering Ren a half-smile and running his hand over the unmarked side of his face. "If I may be honest, this has been a long time coming, my lord."

"Lord Tyke is that bad?"

Dropping his head, Jayce nodded. "Yes."

"Then why did you stay?"

"I didn't know where else I could go."

"To Aleria," Ren suggested.

"And do what?" Jayce asked, a smile creasing the corners of his eyes. "Entertain the court with one-handed juggling?"

The joke managed to bring a smile to Ren's face, if only for a moment. When it faded, it gave way to a hopelessness much greater than before. "What happens now?"

Jayce gave him a curious look and turned to face him. "My lord, I don't think I can answer that question. I'm just a physician. You have the highest rank in the fort. Stag's Run is yours."

"I don't know how to protect these people," Ren said, a tightness forming in his chest. "I don't know how to protect the North."

"We have today and half of tomorrow, still. Take some time to think," Jayce suggested, giving Ren's shoulder a squeeze. "I'll tell the men to give you peace, and whatever you suggest, I'll back it up."

"Thank you."

* * *

The room Ren had been given was cold despite the fire doing its best to push out the chill. This part of the fort was as run down and bare as the rest, a thin layer of dust covering everything except for the bed covers, which had been changed upon his arrival. There were no curtains and no rugs on the floor. Ren's bag was by the bed, along with Anik's. Anik's sword leaned against the wall.

With a heavy sigh, Ren let himself sink down onto the bed, the first time he had gotten off his feet since that morning. Fatigue rolled over him like a wave, his head throbbing.

Ren had known from the beginning that there would be obstacles, but he had never felt like success was out of reach. Until now. He had nothing left, no one to help him. Just a broken fort and a handful of men out of fighting form. He wasn't a leader like Callun or Hellic. Berin, the one man Ren knew he could trust, was in the one place he couldn't reach. Even if he could, it wouldn't be fair to ask Berin to risk the lives of his family, his wife and daughter.

Ren was a royal bastard, destined to a life on the sidelines, a life full of good food, sex, entertainment, and limited responsibilities. A few weeks ago, he had been convinced that his life of luxury would last forever. He had been happy.

Digging a hand into his pocket, he closed his fingers around the delicate silver key. He drew it out and turned it over, tracing the lines in the metal with the tips of his fingers. He knew every curve and crease of it by heart.

'For when you need to escape.'

No matter how long he stared at it, this little moulded piece of metal wasn't going to set him free.

With a heavy sigh, he leaned down and tugged off his boots, dropping them beside the bed. For just one night, he could sleep and pretend none of this was happening. Whatever came tomorrow, he would deal with it then.

* * *

The wind tugged at the grass and made the leaves on the massive tree rustle. Sunlight filtered through them, covering their bodies in specks of light. Hellic's smile was wide and bright, his body dwarfed by the longbow made for grown men twice his size.

Keelan batted his eyelashes, his silken hair falling over his wide hazel eyes as he followed Ren's every movement with adoration.

The apple shone in the light of the sun when Hellic tossed it into the air and caught it again. He handed it to Keelan to place into position, and the small boy hesitated, shy, but complied as Hellic handed Ren the bow. "It's your turn."

Keelan ran through the tall grass back to Ren and covered his eyes.

From behind Ren, Niklas grinned and patted Ren on the shoulder.

Taking the bow from his brother, Ren gripped it tight, but his fingers slipped. When he opened his hand, his palm was covered in blood. So were the bow, the grass, and their clothes. They were all standing in blood, thick crimson washing up against their ankles, an ocean of blood.

Ren's scream tore through the air.

It was pitch black when Ren gasped himself awake. Despite the cold, his body was covered in a layer of sweat. He ripped the blankets off and let them slip to the floor. For a long moment, he simply breathed, but the darkness made his skin crawl with unease, so he pushed himself up and made his stumbling way to the fireplace.

Relighting it took three attempts with his shaking hands. Finally, a small flame started to grow. He was freezing again by the time he returned to the bed and retrieved his blankets, wrapping them around himself like a cocoon. Slowly, the growing flames illuminated the room.

The dream had vanished from his mind the moment he woke, but the feeling of it still lingered. Leaning back against the headboard, he watched the dancing shadows.

What time was it? Sometime after midnight, but with hours until dawn, judging by how dark it was. He barely felt tired now, despite his earlier fatigue.

The firelight danced across shining metal, and Ren turned his gaze to where Anik's sword leaned against the wall, the sheath discarded on the floor as if some curious soldier had wanted to see what kind of weapon the Lowlander carried. Perhaps whoever it was had been surprised to discover that it was Fraynean steel.

Ren hadn't yet gotten a chance to question Anik. Now, it hardly seemed important. Unless Ren came up with some fantastical solution to their problem, they'd all be dead by noon. And if not by noon, then sometime down the road. With Halvard as ruler, Ren doubted anyone who stood against Skarlan soldiers would be spared.

Swinging his legs over the side of the bed, he reached out and closed his hand around the cool handle of Anik's sword, drawing it onto his lap. He hadn't seen Anik use it in a real fight, but he remembered the way he had wielded it during their sparring match and his practice. The slow, precise movements of his body, the sword an extension of himself. It had been harder than it looked. Neither Niklas nor Ren had had much time to practice on the road, not that it would have done Ren much good, anyway. He had pulled his sword against an unarmed man and still nearly lost his life.

Flecks of blood still clung to the blade of the sword just below the crossguard. Anik had drawn his weapon in the woods and skewered the man in front of him. Then Niklas had pried Anik's sword from his hands and knocked him unconscious. Niklas, who couldn't even beat Ren in friendly fights half the time.

Ren's eyes narrowed, a thought growing in his mind, realisations forming and connecting. They made his heart skip and he sat up straighter, grip tightening on Anik's sword.

There was no way Niklas could have disarmed and incapacitated Anik in complete darkness. Anik was much too skilled a fighter, especially against someone like Niklas, who had barely any fighting skills. And there was still that one inconsistency – why would Anik kill a man with whom he had been engaged in what sounded like pleasant conversation with only moments before?

Ren stared at the blade of the sword as if the cold steel could somehow provide him with answers.

Anik'd had no motive for killing that man. The very reason he had followed Ren halfway across the country was to avenge the deaths of his people. Niklas had encouraged Ren to get rid of Anik many times, but Ren had turned him down. Niklas knew he wasn't strong enough to kill Anik himself, so what if getting Ren to dispose of Anik had been his plan all along?

Getting out of bed, Ren discarded the blanket and grabbed his boots, yanking them on without tying the laces. Maybe he was grasping at straws and maybe he was just desperately searching for something that could help him out of this mess, but he had to know the truth.

His boot heels clicked against the stone floors as he marched down the corridor and took the stairs down two at a time. He passed a guard, who jerked awake and was probably relieved that Ren didn't bother reprimanding him for sleeping on the watch.

It was snowing, large flakes drifting to the ground. They landed on his face and melted against the heat of his skin. Crossing the courtyard, Ren made for the cells, taking the two steps down onto a narrow walkway. The cells were shielded from the worst of the weather but were still far more exposed than the royal dungeons in Aleria. The cold made it worse. There was no heat, and at this time of the year, the iron bars were partly covered in a constant layer of frost.

Anik sat in the far corner of his cell, curled up tightly with his arms crossed over his bent head. At the sight of him, Ren stopped. The image of Anik small and bundled up was very much at odds with the image in Ren's head.

"Anik," Ren whispered, wondering if it would startle him, but Anik raised his head slowly, as if he had heard Ren's approach.

He looked wide awake, but his eyes were distant and glassy. His breath misted in the air in front of his face. "Tell me what happened in the woods," Ren continued softly, stepping closer to the bars. They had been in this same situation barely more than a week ago, but this time, Ren wasn't afraid. He wondered if that was a mistake.

"Why should I?" Anik asked, staring at Ren blankly. His voice was rough.

Ren swallowed. "Because I think I've made a mistake. I think I listened to the wrong person."

Anik laughed, a sound entirely devoid of humour. A bit of dried blood was smeared across his temple, making a lock of hair cling to his skin. "Listen to the genius," he mocked, resting his cheek against his forearm. Ren didn't like the joyless smile on his face. Not even when he had been most angry at Ren had he looked like that.

"Anik, I'm sorry, all right? I made a mistake. A big mistake. I should have listened to you. I know you didn't start the attack in the woods and I know you didn't poison the drinks in Sifa's camp." The realization struck him the moment he said it. Of course Anik hadn't done it. But Niklas… Niklas was Ren's best friend. To think that he might have done something so gruesome – no. Ren couldn't get sidetracked now. This was important.

Anik blinked, head cocked to one side, but said nothing, simply kept watching him.

"I need your help," Ren admitted, rubbing his brow with one hand. "Fuck, Anik, I don't know what else you want me to say."

Slowly, Anik stood, movements stiff as if the cold had gotten to his bones. When he approached the bars, Ren could see the hardness in his eyes. "You promised me my freedom. I told you I'd follow you to Stag's Run and then leave. You agreed. I should have known better than to trust your word."

Ren felt what little heat had remained in his face fade and he let his head hang. "I'll do anything. Anything you want."

"Anything?" Anik asked in the same tone.

Ren nodded.

Anik huffed and shook his head. "I didn't know you valued your own life so little."

Ren said nothing. When he looked up, Anik's eyes had softened slightly. He wasn't sure what had caused it, but he'd cling to it like a raft on open waters.

"Someone drew my sword," Anik said, and for a moment, Ren was confused. Then he remembered what he had originally come to ask. "They used it to stab the man in front of me. Before I could move, I was hit over the head. Falling off the wagon was the last thing I remember."

"It was Niklas," Ren said, the words pulling on his heart as he spoke them.

"So, are you going to apologize for talking shit behind my back, too? You two weren't exactly being subtle."

Blowing out a breath, Ren felt his cheeks redden. He ran his hands over them. "I'm sorry."

"You can apologize by letting me out of here," Anik said.

Ren half-ran back across the courtyard to the overseer's office, where the keys to the cells were kept. His boots slipped on the thin layer of snow and he forced himself to slow down just enough not to fall taking the turns. He grabbed a torch from the wall, barely slowing. Anik could help him. He wasn't entirely alone now. Together, they would find a way to win this fight, and then they would at least be alive to figure out what to do next. There would be a way to save Frayne. There had to be a way.

The corridor was empty, only the men stationed outside currently awake. Pushing the door open, Ren placed the torch in the sconce by the wall and went straight to the desk, yanking open the top drawer. Then he froze. He wasn't alone.

He spun around. Niklas was standing in the corner, arms wrapped tightly around himself. Ren's gaze fell on the ring of keys in Niklas' white-knuckled hand.

"I knew you'd come looking for them," Niklas said. His eyes were shadowed. It looked like he hadn't slept at all since Ren had left him on the ramparts.

"Niklas, give me the keys," Ren said, jaw clenching.

"I didn't mean for you to get hurt, I swear," Niklas said, his breath hitching as he inched his way around the room so the desk was between them. "I didn't mean for you to drink that poison. It was an accident. I warned you not to keep drinking."

Ren swallowed hard. A memory came to him, of Niklas bowed over his bed in the tent at the camp, shoulders shaking. It hadn't just been fear for Ren's life, but guilt, too. They had played that game with the sticks, and when Ren had turned to pass Niklas his stones, Niklas had been missing. Moments later, the second keg had been brought out.

"Give me the keys," Ren said more firmly.

"The thing in the forest, it got out of hand. I just wanted you to get rid of him. I didn't know the guy's brother would attack you." Niklas made a choked sound and rubbed his eyes. "I just kept fucking it up. But I can fix it, Ren. I can. If you can just forgive me, we can go back to Aleria. I have influence. My father was Halvard's most trusted general. Halvard loved him like a brother. He'll listen to me. I can get us both protection and we can be okay. Please, Ren."

"You don't understand at all, do you? If you don't understand, I can't explain to you how wrong that would be," Ren said, voice hard. Closing in on Niklas, Ren grabbed his wrist and pried the keys from his fingers.

Niklas didn't resist, just dropped his head. "You always sacrifice yourself for others. Anik is dangerous, Ren. I just want to keep you safe."

Ren's eyes narrowed and he took a step back. "You have an odd way of showing it."

"Don't go," Niklas said, and the look in eyes, so completely heartbroken, was almost enough to melt some of the ice in Ren's heart.

"I have to."

As Ren turned, the sound of horns cut through the silence. Stepping outside, Ren saw that the night was slowly giving way to dawn, colouring the sky a faint grey.

"It's the scouts, my lord." Jayce came towards him from across the courtyard, skidding to a stop alongside him. His hair was ruffled and his jacket was slightly askew, hastily thrown on atop his undershirt. "They've just returned with news about the approaching forces. One hundred and ten men, about five hours away."

Ren looked to the south. Beyond the thick fort walls, Frayne stretched out before them. One hundred and ten Skarlan soldiers riding freely through the heart of his family's country. The mysterious message had been true.

"What are your orders?" Jayce asked.

Ren met his eyes, one warm brown, one milky. It should have been the fort commander here, taking Ren's instructions. Instead, the young physician seemed to have taken on almost every job in the fort, executing each to perfection.

Ren found himself thinking that if they had an entire army of people like Anik and Jayce, they'd be able to retake Frayne and conquer Skarlan in the span of a few days. "Ready the men. All of them," he said.

Jayce nodded. "One more thing."

"Yes?"

"The wagon you arrived with is still inside the fort."

Ren stopped in his tracks, brow furrowing. Ira, Lyle, the driver. "Why haven't they left?"

Jayce shook his head. "They always stay for a few days, and apparently, no one seemed to realize that sending them away before the fort engaged in battle would be a good idea."

Ren groaned, rubbing a hand over his eyes. "We can't send them out there now and risk them running straight into the Skarlans."

"We can keep them safe inside the fort."

Ren nodded. "Do that. And Jayce?" he added.

Jayce stopped and turned halfway back towards Ren. "Yes, my lord?"

"Leave two guards with Niklas," Ren said, holding back a sigh. It pained him to lose active soldiers, but he couldn't risk Niklas trying to hurt someone else. Especially not Anik.

As Jayce left to carry out his orders, Ren went back to the cells.

"Took you a while." Anik was leaning against the edge of the stone wall. His posture was more relaxed, although a hint of discomfort still lingered in the way he held himself.

"I got held up," Ren said, sliding the key into the lock. The gate swung open with a creak. "The Skarlan force is five hours away." He paused, hesitated, then blew out a breath. "Look, I made you a promise." He stopped Anik with a hand on his shoulder. "If you want to leave right now, I won't hold it against you. I owe you that. I just need your advice, anything you can tell me about-"

"Did you honestly think I'd just wander off when there's Skarlan ass to kick?" Anik gave Ren a long, searching look before reaching up and closing his hand around Ren's wrist. The touch was firm, even comforting.

Ren smiled and they let go of each other. It felt like a huge weight had been lifted off his shoulders.

"How many?" Anik asked.

"A hundred and ten," Ren said, leading the way back up into the courtyard. The snow had stopped falling, but it covered the ground like a white blanket.

"That's not an army. More like a company," Anik noted. "They're not expecting much resistance. That's our luck." He glanced briefly at the thin layer of snow at their feet, the sight seeming to surprise him. It made Ren wonder if he had ever even seen snow before.

"Problem is, we aren't much of a resistance," Ren admitted, regaining Anik's attention.

Anik stopped in the middle of the courtyard and looked around. Ren realised this was the first time Anik had seen the condition of the fort. "Talk to me," Anik said.

"We have under thirty soldiers, and even fewer swords. The fort is strong, but not impregnable, and we can't hold it with so few men." He let Anik up the stairs to the ramparts.

"We have the advantage of the slope," Anik noted, taking careful steps to avoid slipping on the steps. "How deep is the moat?"

"Not very," Ren said, leaning over the battlements to look down at the water, which was covered in a thin layer of ice. "You can probably stand upright in it. It's wide, though."

"Men walk slower in water. Archers here and here can pick them off as they wade through," Anik said, pointing to spots along the ramparts on either side of the large gate.

"We need something better," Ren argued.

"Then use that smart little head of yours. It's your fort, isn't it?" Anik said.

"One more thing," Ren said, and withdrew the folded note from inside his coat, handing it to Anik. "A messenger delivered this note to me yesterday. He wouldn't say who sent him, but the warning has proven correct. Would you happen to know any Lowlander with a fox sigil?"

Anik unfolded the note, glancing over the text before his eyes settled on the fox in the corner. Frowning, he shook his head. "We don't use sigils," he said, handing the note back to Ren.

They walked slowly along the ramparts, breaths misting in the early morning air. Ren glanced at Anik, who had returned to studying their surroundings, and he found that it felt good to have Anik at his side again. Despite his sour mood and sharp remarks, Anik had been a reliable companion since their escape from Aleria. Who would have thought Ren would ever feel fond towards a Lowlander?

"Why do Frayne and Skarlan hate each other so much?"

"Hmm?" Ren turned to look at Anik, not expecting the question. "Our countries have been at war for hundreds of years."

Anik looked at him, brow furrowing. He tugged his coat closer around himself against the subtle, chilling breeze. "But how did it start?"

"Well," Ren said, "there's the story about the race to Stag's Run. I'm not sure if it's true, but it's as good an explanation as any."

"What's the story?"

Ren raised his eyebrows, meeting Anik's gaze. "You don't know it? Well, I suppose you wouldn't," he said. Old Skarlan-Fraynean history probably didn't much interest Lowlanders.

Coming to the side of the fort that faced the northward passage, Ren stopped, bracing his arms against the battlements. Next to him, Anik hopped up to sit on the frost-covered stone, one leg on either side, seemingly unfazed by the twenty-meter drop to the ground below.

"A few years after the first settlers came to these lands, before

Frayne and Skarlan had even been formed, a landslide revealed the passage to the North," Ren began, pointing ahead at the sloping path. "The people agreed to send out their strongest warrior to discover this new land, and as a reward, he would be crowned king of his discovery. Two villages both insisted that their chosen warrior was the strongest, so the people decided to send them both. They agreed that the warrior who first planted his flag at the top of the tallest hill would claim all the land within sight. Those warriors' names were Frayne and Skarlan." Ren glanced at Anik, who was watching him intently. Ren had heard this story told so many times, he could probably tell it in his sleep.

"They raced through the passage together, herds of huge stags watching them curiously, unafraid. Finally, when they had been riding all day, the passage ended, opening into a vast, rich land full of animals and plants. But it was late in the day, and the North was freezing cold, so the two warriors decided to share a tent. In an attempt to win Frayne's trust, Skarlan made love to him that night.

"The next morning, before Frayne woke up, Skarlan went out to search for the tallest hill, and he spotted it in the distance. Returning to their camp, Skarlan told Frayne that he had found the hill, and proposed that they claim it together so that they might rule as one. Blinded by his new affection for Skarlan, Frayne agreed. Skarlan offered to pack up the camp and told

Frayne to go ahead to the hill, but sent him off in the wrong direction. As soon as Frayne was out of sight, Skarlan ran to the hill and planted his flag. From the top of his own, much smaller hill, Frayne spotted Skarlan and rushed to meet him, demanding an explanation. Skarlan revealed his deceit, telling Frayne that he had always planned on ruling the North alone.

"Overwhelmed by anger, heartbreak, and sadness, Frayne drew his sword and impaled Skarlan, killing him. He planted his own flag where Skarlan's had stood and returned to the settlers. When he arrived, his village worshipped him as a hero. But Skarlan's family demanded to know what had become of their own warrior. Not wishing to cause bad blood between their families, Frayne told them that Skarlan had been killed by a massive bear in the night, and that Frayne had found his body in the morning, already cold. Then, a member of Skarlan's family saw the blood on Frayne's blade and accused him of the murder.

"It started a feud between the villages, and the feud turned into a war. Borders were drawn, forts and castles were built. The first Skarlan king killed Frayne. Frayne's son declared war to avenge his father, and the rest is history." Ren looked across at Anik, curious to see his reaction.

Anik had his head tilted, one eyebrow raised. "It sounds a bit unbelievable."

That triggered a laugh from Ren, who shrugged. "Maybe it is. Maybe it isn't. Regardless of how true it is, it started a century-long war."

"I thought there was a peace agreement," Anik said.

"There was. My grandfather fought the last battle against Skarlan. It was a disaster. A terrible drought killed over half the armies on both sides. I think everyone was sick of fighting at that point."

"The peace didn't last long," Anik noted.

Ren huffed, a bitter sound. "Fucking Skarlans."

"You can say that again. And all the while your people fought and argued, Lowlanders lived peacefully just south of your blood-stained forts and castles." Anik bowed his head, picking at a dry patch of lichen. "Until the Skarlans found us."

Ren watched Anik's face. Halvard had hurt Anik's family just like he had hurt Ren's. Ren supposed that if anyone understood why this fight was so important, it was Anik.

When the settlers had split the land into two nations, both countries had gathered as many resources as they could to fortify themselves against each other. It didn't surprise Ren that the Skarlans had deemed the hardy and strong Lowlanders a valuable human resource despite their reputation.

"So that's the North," Anik said, angling his chin towards the winding slopes before them.

Ren nodded. "Yes, that's the North. Or, it's that way, at least. Stag's Run passage is many miles long."

"Those aren't exactly stags, though," Anik said, pointing to the

219

herd of cattle grazing on the slope. A slight smirk tugged at the corner of his lips. "So what do you say, skahli? Lord of Cattle's Run?"

Ren rolled his eyes. "They use the cattle for-" He paused.

Cattle's Run. The idea almost knocked the breath from his lungs. He gripped Anik's arm, making him flinch. "I think I know how we can defeat the army."

CHAPTER TEN

Ren led the way to the passage gates, Anik and Jayce on his heels. A pair of soldiers pushed open the large gates and several curious cows lifted their heads.

"We don't have very many soldiers, but we have cattle," Ren said, the frost cracking under his boots as he strode forward. The animals watched him curiously, trying to determine whether he had food, then lowered their heads to nibble the short grass.

"How many are there?" Ren asked, turning to face Jayce.

"Thirty-one, I think. What exactly do you intend for the cows to do?" Jayce asked, looking between Ren and Anik.

It was Anik who answered. "The moat."

"Exactly," Ren said. "When the Skarlans approach the gate to ram it, we simply open it wide, herd the cattle out onto the bridge and push the soldiers into the water. Then all the archers have to worry about is picking them off in the moat."

"The moat is wide and the attackers will move slowly through the water. However many Skarlan soldiers manage to make it through the gate after the cattle have passed over the bridge, there should be few enough for our soldiers on the inside to handle them," Anik said.

"Using cows as soldiers," Jayce said, running his hand through his short, dark curls. "That's a wild plan. Worthy of a Lowlander. No offence." He glanced from Ren to Anik, a soft flush reaching his cheeks.

Anik simply chuckled. "It'll work."

They prepared for the attack in the fort armoury. With the equipment in varying states of repair, hardly anyone could be provided with a full set of armour. The soldiers defending the courtyard got most of it, since they'd be bearing the brunt of the fighting. The archers were provided with as many helmets and leather breastplates as they had, and the rest was makeshift. Ren had lined the soldiers up in the courtyard and filled them in on the plan. Ren could hear them murmur nervously to each other. He wondered how many of them had fought a battle before. Most of them looked like seasoned fighters, but there were a few young ones in between, strapping into their armour with pale faces and jaws clenched tight.

Ren strapped a pair of bracers to his forearms. Considering he wasn't planning on engaging the enemy head-on, the amount of armour he wore felt irrelevant. A part of him was glad for it, but another part couldn't help but feel like there were men who needed it more than he did. Despite his own feelings, everyone seemed to have unanimously agreed that their prince – bastard or not – should be well-protected.

The men hadn't been as considerate towards Anik. They had tolerated him walking free, but when Ren declared that Anik would be leading the defence of Stag's Run alongside him, many of them had balked. Ren had silenced them with a strength of conviction he had always thought was reserved for men like King Callun. The soldiers had immediately complied, but they still sent Anik nervous glances whenever they passed.

Anik wasn't the only source of apprehension. The size of the approaching army was no secret. The men were following a stranger into a fight they could easily lose, and Ren wouldn't have blamed them if they had decided to back out. But they were all still here, preparing for battle with clenched jaws and hard eyes. They knew as well as anyone what was at stake. The news of Halvard in the heart of their country had sent ripples of shock through Stag's Run. Protecting the fort was now more important than ever. Ren had to give it to them: however slack they had become, they were prepared to fight today. Not one of them had spoken a single word of doubt. No one had questioned his authority. Ren couldn't help but think that perhaps they should.

He would have, if he'd been in their shoes.

The last of the soldiers left the armoury to take up position along the ramparts and in the courtyard, leaving Anik and Ren alone for a few, quiet moments. The silence before the storm.

Ren sat down on the nearest bench and stretched his legs. "I've known Niklas since we were children," he said. The leather greaves were unfamiliar and tight around his calves. "I was so sure I could trust him. I've never had a reason not to. He's always had my back."

"Rolling over for the Skarlan king," Anik said, spitting on the ground and tugging on the straps of his leather breastplate. It was the only piece of protection he wore, a worn thing with faded engraved antlers along the top, sliced through by old cuts and scrapes. His sword was strapped to his hip, although they had no shields to spare. "It's disgusting. You don't betray the people you call your family."

It was almost strange not to be the focus of Anik's insults for once, although Ren was sure he still had plenty to spare. Maybe Anik could sense his unease. No matter the reason, Ren appreciated it.

"The Skarlans are his family," Ren said quietly. "He was born there."

Anik shook his head. "Blood doesn't equal family."

Taking a deep breath, Ren found that his hand shook as he closed it around the hilt of his brother's sword, a comforting presence at his side. "Do you think we'll be okay?"

"I don't know," Anik said, taking a seat on the bench beside him. "Speculation is useless. All we can do is give it our best shot."

"I'm terrible in a fight. You know that."

Anik smiled a little. "Yeah, you are. Good thing you're also a prince and won't be on the front lines where all the real bad shit goes down. Just remember to keep your guard up and watch for arrows and I'm sure you'll be fine."

Ren frowned. "Anik, I'm serious."

"So am I. The men will keep you safe. It's not your job to hack and slash, it's your job to give orders and keep the fight under control."

Meeting Anik's steady brown eyes, Ren suppressed a sigh. "I've never done that, either."

Anik's laugh was quiet, a welcome sound. "I'll help you with that. Come on, get your ass off that bench. Your men are waiting."

The fort was buzzing with activity as they left the armoury, even if their army was only a shadow of what it should have been. Two soldiers guarded Niklas, and with Ren and Anik added to the roster, they were still only twenty-nine souls. They'd be outnumbered almost four to one.

As Ren watched, soldiers moved into position, led by men who were led by him. Ren Frayne, the bastard prince, leading his first fight against Skarlans, during a Fraynean-Skarlan peace agreement, deep inside Fraynean territory.

In truth, Ren was leading the fight in name only. Of everyone gathered in Stag's Run, he was likely the most inexperienced on a battlefield. His only job was to tell these men when to strike. It was up to the soldiers to win the day. Still, Ren began to realise, that didn't make him any less important. He had the final say. The responsibility was ultimately his, and he wasn't sure how he felt about that.

The sound of the alarm horns echoed between the mountainsides as the lookouts in the towers spotted the Skarlan advance riders ahead.

"Archers at the ready. Gather the cattle." Anik's orders were passed across the courtyard. The wind tugged on his hair, pulling a few strands loose from the leather band that held it back from his face. Ren absently wondered if he ever let his hair down. Ren heard the subtle sound of men raising their weapons. Their faces were hard with a mix of determination and nervous anticipation.

"I really hope I'm not about to get all these people killed," Ren said quietly as they ascended the steps that led to the ramparts where archers were crouched behind the battlements, Anik right behind him. A few glanced back at him as they approached, but most of them were focused on the threat ahead.

"You aren't," Anik said, fingertips playing with the hilt of his sword, a restless motion. "The plan is sound. Trust it."

226

Ren looked across at him. He wasn't sure at what point this sense of camaraderie had developed between them, but regardless of what had triggered it, Ren appreciated the break from the constant hostility. Especially if this was going to be their last day alive. All around them, men and women stood with straight backs and their hands clasped firmly around their weapons. Any one of them could die today, Ren thought. No battle had ever been fought without casualties. It turned his stomach to think about.

The riders, when they approached, were scattered. The message and the scouts had both been right – the Skarlans clearly weren't expecting much resistance, approaching with no sense of guard or battle formation. When they saw the archers on the ramparts, however, they gathered. Ren heard shouted orders from their commander.

The group of soldiers stopped just out of shooting range and a single rider came forward, halting her horse in front of the stone bridge.

The fort was deathly silent, only the Frayne standards snapping in the wind above the keep towers making any sound. Even the cattle were quiet, herded close together in the courtyard below by a small group of soldiers on horseback.

The Skarlan rider's voice carried when she spoke, breath misting in front of her face. "King Halvard of Skarlan, protector of the Fraynean throne, demands your surrender. If you give up this fort willingly, the lives of all soldiers within its walls will be spared and you will be allowed safe passage to your homes and families. The only condition is that the bastard prince and his slave must be delivered to us."

"If Skarlan rules Frayne and the North," Anik said, voice hushed, "then the rest of these lands will be subject to the same cruelty as the Lowlands."

The messenger waited, horse pawing at the ground impatiently. "This is your final warning. We will attack and bring Stag's Run to heel."

"Ready with the cattle," Ren said over his shoulder, voice hushed. The order was repeated down the stairs until it reached the riders surrounding the animals in the courtyard. They pushed their horses in closer, making the beasts lift their heads in an attempt to press forward against the closed gates.

Finding that no reply was forthcoming, the messenger spun her horse and galloped back towards the Skarlan army. As Ren watched, the soldiers regrouped into two columns and advanced, the hooves of their animals digging into the wet ground. Heavy chains were brought forward, metal links shining in the sunlight. They were preparing to pull the gate off its hinges. They weren't expecting Ren's soldiers to simply open them willingly.

Ren shared a glance with Anik. Anik was smiling, a wicked grin on his face. How anyone could look so at ease in the face of death was beyond him.

The first column of soldiers marched onto the bridge with

their shields raised above their heads. Behind them, the second column lined up, ready to breach the fort. There were so many of them. Ren's archers tensed the strings of their bows, but didn't fire.

Ren leaned over the battlements, standing on the tips of his toes to watch the soldiers below approach the gate. A hand – Anik's – twisted in the back of his coat, ready to yank him back at the first sight of an enemy archer taking aim.

Below, the chains were passed to the soldiers in front, hands raised to hook the giant links onto the thick wooden gate.

"Now! Open the gate!" Ren shouted, and for a few seconds, the creak of the heavy wooden gate swinging open was the only sound to be heard.

Even from this high up, Ren could see the faces of the Skarlan soldiers change from surprise to fear. Then shouts filled the air, the men stumbling backwards and falling over each other.

The herders behind the cattle heeled their horses forward, snapping whips above their heads. The cattle startled and charged towards the only possible exit, barrelling into the soldiers gathered on the narrow bridge.

The cattle ploughed through the line of soldiers like a living battering ram. They tossed their heads and slammed their horns into the heads and bodies of soldiers with sickly cracks of broken bones. The first splash of a body hitting water was soon followed by many more, and the riders at the foot of the bridge yanked their horses backward or attempted to wheel away from the herd of stampeding cattle. One horse reared up, throwing its rider from the saddle. Those that didn't fall into the water were trampled by the massive animals.

"Archers, fire at will," Ren shouted, and heard his command relayed down the lines, followed by the snap of bowstrings against wood as the archers let their arrows fly. Many arrows found their targets in the necks, heads, and torsos of soldiers scrambling to get out of the water. The cattle fanned out, continuing down the slope and forcing the second column of riders to break and move out of their way.

"Form a defence line in the courtyard," Anik shouted, grabbing a bow and tossing it to Ren, who caught it with both hands. Below, Skarlan soldiers were falling like flies even as more tried to press on through the gate and into the fort. As Ren watched, Anik drew his sword from his hip and turned. He leapt down the stairs like a cat and joined the others below. Shoulder to shoulder with the Fraynean soldiers, Anik held their invaders at bay, shouting commands to the men around him to keep the line tight.

Grabbing an arrow from one of the boxes on the ramparts, Ren nocked it, drew the bow, and took aim. He chose a target. The man was trying to pull himself back onto the bridge, but gave up when a horse thundered past and decided to go for the bank instead. His movements were panicked as he stumbled, sliding in the mud and struggling in the icy cold. Ren hesitated, hand shaking on the bow. All he had to do was release. Just let the arrow fly and bury itself into flesh with a sickly rip that would mix blood with water.

He couldn't.

On both sides of him, archers sent their arrows into the bodies of the men below. Almost two dozen had fallen, spilled blood colouring the snow a hideously lurid red and the water dark like wine. Clutching the bow in one hand, he turned to look down into the courtyard. Blood was flowing there, too, and not only Skarlan blood. Fraynean soldiers had fallen, their comrades forced to step over their bodies as they fought to hold the line. No grand story of heroic battles could have prepared Ren for this raw and brutal carnage, for the cries of injured men mixing with the shouts of exertion and sharp clangs of steel. The only comfort was that the Skarlans were suffering far more casualties than the Fraynean soldiers.

A hard tug on his arm made Ren yelp, and he stumbled aside just as an arrow bounced off the stone beside his head.

"Excuse me, my lord." The young man who had tugged him aside looked at Ren with wide, blue eyes. He was barely older than Hellic, strands of black hair sweat-damp despite the cold.

"Thank you," Ren said, oddly out of breath. The young man turned, gripping his bow tight and leaning against the battlements once more, eager to throw himself back into the fray. More arrows followed the first and Ren staggered back, out of their range.

Ren tossed his bow. It was no use to him. Instead, he drew Hellic's sword, grip tight on the hilt.

"Ren!"

He whipped around. Anik had left the defence line and scaled the stairs. He wasn't looking at Ren, but was scanning the courtyard below where their men were holding strong. "Where's their commander? I just saw him, but now he's gone."

"Is he inside?" Ren called back, following Anik's gaze. He searched the crowd for a gilded helmet or a flowing cloak, any sign of elevated status, but all he saw were the blood-stained uniforms of men in white and grey.

"No."

"Maybe he's dead."

"He's not dead!" Anik shouted, and Ren saw frustration in his eyes when they looked at each other.

"Stop, in the name of the King." The voice cut through the shouts of men and the clatter of weapons.

Ren spun around to look out over the battlements.

From the back of the severely diminished Skarlan army came the commander in his silver armour. In front of him sat a boy, pressed against the commander's chest with the man's blade at his throat. A young boy, with dark hair and a furious expression, despite the streaks of dried tears on his cheeks.

Ren's heart skipped a beat, then another. For a long, horrifying moment, it felt like his body had forgotten how to function, until all his senses returned to him in a rush that left him breathless. "Thais!" The breaking of his own voice, loud in his ears, almost startled him as he turned to run towards the stairs and the gate below, but Anik seemed to come out of nowhere and locked his arms around his torso, keeping him in place.

"Halt!" Anik's voice was a roar, even louder than Ren's had been, and almost instantly, the sounds of the fighting died down around them. Fraynean soldiers pulled back, looking up in bewilderment. The Skarlan soldiers kept their swords raised, moving in through the open gates.

"Surrender, or the boy dies." The commander's voice sliced through this new silence like an arrow through flesh, but Ren's own heart beating loud in his ears almost drowned it out.

A blur of movement made Ren turn. Anik was no longer holding him in place, but was reaching for Ren's discarded bow and nocking an arrow in one fluid motion.

"What are you doing?" Ren hissed, closing his hand around Anik's wrist.

"I can take him out."

"No! From this distance, you could hit my brother."

Their eyes met. Slowly, Anik lowered his bow.

Ren let his gaze sweep over the courtyard, over the remains of the Skarlan army. Victory had been within reach. A few more

minutes, and Stag's Run would have been secured. He tried
frantically to think of a way to turn this around, to outsmart the
commander, save Thais and recover their victory. As the seconds
passed, it became terribly clear to him that there was no
alternative. Just like that, it was over.

"My lord." Jayce's voice made Ren flinch. He came up the
stairs towards them.

Ren turned slowly with blood still rushing in his ears.

"You should surrender."

Ren's jaw worked. "You... Our soldiers..."

"We'll be all right," Jayce assured him, voice hushed in the
silence. He placed his hand on Ren's shoulder and pulled him
close. The scents of sweat and blood clung to his body. "Save
your brother."

Ren locked eyes with Anik. The Lowlander looked furious,
but the anger wasn't directed at Ren. He gave a single, stiff nod.
"Let them through."

All along the ramparts, archers lowered their bows. Ren
sheathed his sword with a trembling hand.

A deathly silence descended over Stag's Run as the Skarlan
commander rode through the gate with Thais against his chest,
the remaining Skarlan soldiers trailing behind. Several of them
sneered at Fraynean soldiers and spat at their feet. The Skarlan
force was a shadow of what it had been, but Ren felt no relief at
the sight.

Descending the stairs on wooden legs, Ren tried to catch Thais' eyes, to try to get some sense of whether he was all right, but his brother refused to meet his gaze as the commander came to a stop in the centre of the courtyard. If Thais was here, then Halvard's plans had changed. Whatever the reason, it couldn't be good news. The fear that Ren might have to watch this man slit his brother's throat and discard his body on the icy cobblestones made it hard to breathe.

The commander looked left and right, then waved a hand to his men. "Kill the archers."

The snapping of bowstrings against wood sounded before Ren could even comprehend those three terrible words. Around him, men fell from the ramparts like sacks of grain and hit the ground with sickly sounds.

"You promised," Ren screamed, running for the commander, hand closed tight around the hilt of his sword. "You promised they wouldn't be hurt!" He didn't even get to draw the blade halfway from its sheath before several pairs of arms locked around his and forced him down onto the hard stone. A second later, a fist aimed at his jaw sent him scrambling and he spat blood onto the ground, fingers numb from cold as he pushed himself back upright.

"It's too late for that," the commander said.

"Father!" A small figure darted from the shadows of the keep and out into the courtyard. The sound of his panicked breaths

235

filled the air, the boy's sobs the only sound to be heard as he threw himself towards one of the dead archers on the ground. A Skarlan soldier caught the boy with an arm over his chest and hauled him back towards the centre of the courtyard. Lyle's face was streaked with tears as he kicked and thrashed in the soldier's grip.

"Let him go." Anik's voice was raised to be heard over the boy's cries and Ren turned to see dozens of swords aimed at the Lowlander. "He's just a boy."

The commander watched the scene with curious fascination, like a child playing with an ant hill. At the front of his saddle, Thais sat with his eyes trained on his own hands, the knife still pressed to his throat.

With a furious cry, Lyle drew a short dagger from his belt and drove it into the stomach of the guard holding him. The man let out a choked sound, dropping the boy on the ground with an expression of pure shock on his face. Dark blood trickled from a deep gash in his abdomen.

The commander's eyes narrowed and he gestured for a soldier, who stepped forward, raising his sword.

"No!" The word tore its way out of Ren's throat as he threw himself against the hands of the men holding him, but it was too late.

Dark rivulets of blood ran down Lyle's front as the soldier sliced his throat with the edge of his sword.

A terrible scream pierced the air. On the stairs of the keep, Ira fell to her knees, hands tearing out strands of her own hair. Two Fraynean soldiers held her back, keeping her from throwing herself into death after her brother.

Waves of shock crashed through Ren, the sharp scent of blood heavy on the air. Lyle had collapsed against the soldier's chest, head lolling to the side. Ren's couldn't take his eyes off the gruesome sight. Not again. Not-

"Restrain the bastard, the slave, and what remains of their men and prepare them for transport," the commander ordered. He rode his horse up to Ren, so close Ren could feel the heat radiating off the animal's body. "We're taking them to Fort Endurance. Lord Nathair will oversee their execution."

Nathair, King Halvard's advisor, had been at the party. Through the fog in his mind, Ren remembered him as the man who had rushed onto the stage, stopped Anik's performance, and revealed the bloody knife that had sealed their fate. Dread filled his gut, heavy and sickening. He looked over his shoulder at Anik, whose face had paled. Behind him, Niklas stood at the foot of the stairs of the keep, free of the guards Ren had sent to watch him. Like Thais, he wouldn't meet Ren's eyes.

The soldiers hauled Ren to his feet. The commander stopped his horse in front of the stone steps, taking Thais with him into the keep.

Above them, dark clouds rolled in. It began to snow.

To be continued...

ACKNOWLEDGEMENTS

This trilogy started as a wild and seemingly overambitious project in May 2015. Never before had I taken on something so large and detailed. Being more of a visual artist than a writer, and tackling this project in a language that wasn't my own made it a daunting task. But the massive amount of support I received from online communities before the first book was even published, completely blew me away. Hundreds of people signed up to follow the progress of this story, and so much of my motivation came from the support and encouragement of everyone who wanted to see this book complete.

I owe so much to Thea Davison, who spent countless hours on Skype listening to my endless rambles, frustrations and ideas, and who read thousands of words of this story in an effort to help me polish dialogue and grammar. I couldn't have done this without you.

To my lovely editor, Sarah Wright, who spent her free time making sure the final story was as good as it could be. Your help was invaluable.

To Nerime, who's positive encouragement and excitement for these characters never failed to make me smile.

To MariaM, Kendra Frost, Josefin W, Francesca Kaddatz and the others who believed in this story enough to support it on Patreon. It really means the world to me.

And to everyone else who shared news of this story with their friends online and followed it's progress: You have made this an incredible experience for me.

LIST OF CHARACTERS

ALERIA

CALLUN – King of Frayne

HELLIC – Crown Prince of Frayne

THAIS – Prince of Frayne, the youngest

REN – The Queen of Frayne's bastard son, the oldest

BERIN – Captain of the Royal Guard of Frayne

NIKLAS – A member of the Fraynean court

LADY CAVAZÉ – Lady of a fort by the sea

KEELAN – Hellic's personal slave

LORD AEVIS – A lord with blond hair and a hook nose

DANALI – Callun's personal slave

AVERY – Thais' personal slave

ADVISOR SELVA – A royal advisor

STAG'S RUN

LORD TYKE – Lord of Stag's Run

JAYCE – Physician at Stag's Run

LYLE – A young boy, son of a soldier

IRA – Lyle's older sister

SKARLANS

HALVARD – King of Skarlan

EVALYNE – Crown Princess of Skarlan

NATHAIR - Halvard's Royal Advisor

LOWLANDERS

ANIK – A slave gifted to Ren by King Halvard

ILIAS – A young slave owned by the butcher Rowland

SIFA – Leader of a Lowlander refugee camp in Frayne

LEINE – Sifa's most trusted

OTHERS

LORD SCYAN – A young lord from Isleya

ROWLAND – A butcher

LORD ELGRIN – The ruler of Draxia

LORD ALASANDER – Lord Elgrin's brother

Connect with Zaya Feli:

Twitter: https://twitter.com/zayafeli

Tumblr: http://zayafeli.tumblr.com/

Author Email: zayafeli@gmail.com

Website: https://zayafeli.wixsite.com/stories